Weeping Dune

by Serenity McLean

Weeping Dune

Published by Dome Tree Publishing
ISBN 978-0-9937314-6-4
© Serenity McLean, 2016
All Rights Reserved

Author's Note

*When they walk through the Valley of Weeping, it will become a
place of refreshing springs.*
The autumn rains will clothe it with blessings.
*They will continue to grow stronger, and each of them will appear
before God in Jerusalem.*
For the Lord God is our sun and our shield.
He gives us grace and glory.
*The Lord will withhold no good thing from those who do what is
right.*
Psalms 84:6–7, 11

Weeping Dune is the story of a life turned around. The main character
Jules finds herself running from a desperate situation, but she is not
sure if she can handle to loneliness of her escape. In her dark abyss she
encounters God and He puts her on a path that changes everything.

I've experienced desperate circumstances and the feeling of existing
in a black hole without hope. But then God stepped in and life hasn't
been the same since. I've also made the difficult decision to live in
loneliness over living in a painful relationship. I'm sure there are many
others with a similar story. I hope to encourage you that God wants to
provide an abundant life of peace and joy, not a life of fear and emptiness.

I hope this story inspires you to see all of God's provision in your life,
and appreciate the gift of family and friends.

Enjoy and blessings,

Credits

Thanks to the many who encouraged me along the way since my first book *Memory of Memories*. I continue to appreciate my mom who encourages and is my biggest fan – love you, Mom.

Thanks to friends who continue to encourage, give feedback and patiently wait between writing spurts to meet. And a note of appreciation to all who have written such great reviews. You inspire me!

Thanks to my Hawaiian pastor JD Farag, for being my online pastor, graciously consenting to being a character in the Glass Darkly series of stories, and contributing a message to all my readers.

My great thanks to my editor Janet Dimond who both passed along improvement ideas and painstakingly pointed out all my errors.

Biggest thanks to my Lord who leads and directs in all things.

Contents

Weeping Dune

Chapter 1 | Intolerable

Tuesday, June 13

She hid in the dark bathroom, sobbing. Waiting. Listening. Quiet finally ruled the hotel room for at least an hour. She came to a decision. Cowering in the darkness gave her plenty of time to think. She finally had enough. The rocky relationship had crossed her line. Anders scared her. Now she needed to wait until he fell into a drunken sleep to quietly slip away.

Some vacation, she thought bitterly. *How could it go so badly on the first day?* She thought they both committed to use this vacation to get their relationship back on track. She pledged to let go of the pain and give her whole heart to a new start. Instead she found herself with fresh emotional wounds, and if Anders hadn't been drunk, he probably would've landed that first blow.

She had struggled a long time with his psychological attacks, thinking she was weak and too sensitive. She thought she needed to toughen up. And she would've continued trying to shrug off his targeted torment, except assault crossed her line. She would not be anyone's punching bag.

Sitting in the dark on the cold bathroom floor, she thought it a perfect echo of her broken heart. A room with a toilet was the perfect place for her to call an end to the relationship. Finally, she stood up, stiffly, strength and fear pounding in her head.

She listened at the door, holding her breath to hear every sound. She was sure she heard heavy, steady breathing. She listened for another minute. She needed him to be in a deep enough sleep to grab her purse and at least her carry-on.

There was a deep snore, then back to heavy breathing. Quietly, slowly, she opened the door and peeked through the crack. The room was slightly lighter than the bathroom. He must have left the curtains open. *That should provide enough light to find my stuff and get out.*

With a pounding heart she decided it was now or never. She did not want to face him in the morning. It would be filled with a twisting of the truth and another compromise on her part. *Never again.*

With the door partly open, she paused briefly, ready to close it quickly if needed. All she heard was his deep, rhythmical breathing. She stepped through the vanity area and waited another five heartbeats before looking around the corner to the bed.

Still fully clothed Anders had passed out on top of the covers. She slowly let out her breath not realizing she had been holding it. She took a moment to let out a couple of slow, deep breaths. She stepped lightly across the room and gently picked up her purse off the desk. Then she headed to the sitting area to grab her carry-on. She stuffed her travel clothes and runners back in and gingerly zipped it closed enough to carry. She stopped to look at her large case with all her clothes, and wondered if it would be too much to handle when trying to make a quick escape. She would have no clothes if she didn't take it, and Anders would likely leave it behind.

Once she tucked her purse in the carry-on and grabbed her suitcase, she tiptoed to the door. She knew the bright light of the hall would flood the room and wanted to move quickly, but steadily. It would not be good if she accidentally bumped her bags on the door or walls on the way out. Again, she paused to breathe out the tension.

As quietly as she could, she turned the lock. Wincing, she heard the inevitable clunk and glanced back to listen for any change in Anders' breathing. Satisfied the noise had not roused him, she carefully turned the knob and slowly pulled the door open a crack. Ears on full alert she heard voices coming down the hall. Softly she closed the door, but held the knob open, ready to quickly slip out after the people passed.

Breathing through her mouth she listened to the voices become louder. They laughed about something. She counted to 30 to be sure they were gone and then slowly pulled the door open a crack again. Listening, she heard nothing.

She opened the door enough for her and her bags to pass, then quietly closed the door behind her. She heard a loud snort as Anders gasped for air. Worried he would wake up she dashed for the end of the hall and took the emergency stairwell.

She ran down ten flights of stairs then paused to listen. The stairwell was quiet. She thought it best to slow down and enter the lobby looking cool and collected. So she took the final two flights of stairs at a more normal pace.

With determination she opened the door to the main floor and made her way to the front desk to ask for a cab. The man at the desk said it would be about five minutes. She thanked him and headed outside to wait. The evening was lovely and warm, and under normal circumstances she would have enjoyed the fragrance of the flowers lingering in the humid air. But tonight the scent didn't register. She paced nervously, glancing occasionally into the hotel lobby to be sure Anders was not coming for her.

Finally, she saw the taxi turn into the hotel entrance and waved. He pulled up and she hopped in, quickly pulling the door shut behind her. The cabbie asked where she was going. *Where am I going?* She hadn't thought this far ahead. She'd only focused on the getting out part, not the getting away part. "To the airport, please."

Chapter 2 | Escape

Juleena considered the various possibilities of where to hide out for her four-week vacation, and decided leaving town quickly was more important than location. She would choose based on the next available flights. Positive Anders would return home as soon as he figured she left, she didn't want to go back to New York City. She couldn't deal with him. She needed time and space to get her head together. She'd booked four weeks' holiday from work and decided to take that time to figure things out. She just needed a place where Anders couldn't find her.

It was almost 4 a.m. when she got to the airport and found it nearly empty. A couple of female agents waited at the desks, a guy ran a floor cleaner and one security stood guard at the far end. Putting on her best casual and cool demeanour, she approached the older of the two agents. "Hi. I'm looking to get out of town. Having a spot of man trouble and need a break. What domestic flights do you have first thing this morning?"

The woman had a kind look about her eyes. "No worries, dear. Let me take a look at what flights have seats available. Will you be looking for first class?"

She looked down at the evening gown she was still wearing. "No, any seat will do."

The woman clicked away at the keyboard and said, "We have a 5:15 to Houston, a 5:25 to St. Louis, a 5:30 to New York City, another 5:30 to Boston, a 5:40 to Charleston, a 5:50 to Denver, a – "

"Wait, Charleston, South Carolina? What time was that one again?"

"It boards at 5:20 and is scheduled to leave at 5:40."

As soon as she heard Charleston, she had a flash of memory. "That's the one. I have one suitcase to check in."

She passed through security, and headed for the bathroom to change out of her evening dress into the clothes she travelled in the day before – a comfortable pair of jeans and T-shirt. She stopped for a chai latte and headed for the gate. A few people were already waiting there. She selected a seat against the windows where she could watch everyone coming down the hall. She was glad to have made it this far, but wouldn't feel safe until the doors of the plane closed and she was on her way.

She had fond memories of spending her summers with her grandmother in Edisto Beach, on a coastal island between Charleston and Hilton Head. Her grammy lived in a small home at the north end of Point Street looking southeast into the Atlantic Ocean, and she happily spent most of her time on the beach. A wave of loneliness and longing weighed on her already burdened heart. Her grammy had passed away when she was 14. Every time she smelled crab or shrimp, she remembered how she loved her grammy's cooking. Smiling she thought, *Grammy was always trying to fatten me up.*

She'd never told Anders about her time at her grammy's. He wasn't interested in her stories. As she thought about it, she realized he was truly only interested in himself.

Yes, I'll rent a car in Charleston and head down to Edisto Island. It would be good to be somewhere familiar.

Finally, they called for preboarding. She knew she would be safe and free of Anders in a few minutes. Although she knew in her head he was probably still sleeping, her heart still held onto the fear he would somehow find her at the last minute.

Her leg bounced as she anxiously waited to board. She watched as the advanced boarding completed, then gathered her things and headed for the gate. She'd chosen a seat at the back of the plane, thinking there would be fewer people and she could board first. While waiting for the first passengers to board, she sent Anders a text to let him know she was okay and that she wouldn't be back. She then shut off her phone. She knew he'd call and she wasn't ready to talk.

The flight from Washington, D.C. was a short 90 minutes. She left behind late spring and welcomed summer as soon as she left the airport. She closed her eyes, relaxed her shoulders and took in a deep breath of the warm, humid air. The air reached into her depths and blew out her anxiety.

She avoided using any shared account for her purchases and rented a car using her own Visa. Once clear of the airport, she headed south to Citadel Mall. She needed some clothes and supplies for her beachside vacation, and a good collection of books to read. She packed for a vacation in and around Washington in late spring, not the warm summer of Edisto. Thankfully she could easily afford new clothes. She earned a healthy income as an accounting consultant for a project firm.

Sitting in the parking lot, waiting for the mall to open, she had time to think. She felt torn. Her heart was broken. She mourned the loss of companionship – or relationship – or whatever it was. On the other hand, the breakup was a long time coming. Breathing in the pleasant air of South Carolina, her future felt a bit brighter. This was not a time to be waffling. *I've made a good decision. Now I need to be strong enough to see it through.*

She knew there would be some hard days when she would feel alone and lonely. But at least for the moment her heart felt lighter. It just seemed right to be going back to a place she loved.

Her mother died giving birth to her and her father really had little time for her. But she loved her grammy and her grammy loved her too. They spent wonderful summers together exploring the island, collecting shells, working in the kitchen and sipping sweet tea on the porch swing. And she loved all the wisdom her grammy tried to pour into her life like, "Work hard, treat others softly and make plenty of room for yourself." Well, she would take the next four weeks to make that room.

She bought enough beach clothes to get her through the next month. She stopped at the bookstore to find some good summer reading and picked out ten books. While in the bookstore she saw a journal with an image of the moon at night on the cover and on a whim picked it up. She thought she would journal her thoughts to help with her resolve. She stopped at a bank to get some cash and a tourist trap to pick up some beach supplies.

In the parking lot she looked up vacation rentals on the Internet and made a few calls, but found all the places fully booked. On the last call she spoke with a young woman who mentioned her cousin had a place that was not listed. The owner just finished renovations and she thought it might be ready to rent.

She called asking to speak with Cassandra Harris. A happy voice answered. Juleena explained her situation, how she got the number and asked if the rental was available. Laughing, Cassandra said her cousin would be the best thing for her new business. It was one of three one-bedroom apartments with a kitchen, sitting room and shared veranda located on Neptune Street, just a block from the beach. After asking about rates she thought it sounded perfect. She rented it for the full four weeks. Once on the road again, it took an hour to get onto the island and to her temporary home.

Chapter 3 | Intersection

A tall, slim blonde greeted her in the driveway and took her upstairs onto the veranda of a stilt house. She'd always loved the look of these coastal homes. They chatted about this being a new business for Cassandra. She lived next door and bought this property when it went up for sale. Her brother did all the renovations and she was the decorator. Juleena loved it and thought it had the look of a Malaysian plantation. She was grateful the price included linens and towels.

She thought she would head to the beach for the afternoon, but once Cassandra left her to unpack, she lay down for a few moments and woke up later in the afternoon. She decided to go out for dinner that first night, then get in groceries the next morning. She noticed several brochures and information sheets on the kitchen counter and took a look for information on local restaurants.

Edisto Beach was a small town offering a limited restaurant selection. Looking over the short list, she thought Grover's Bar and Grill looked good. She enjoyed the atmosphere, the local crab specialty and that Chef Heather came out to greet her to check that she enjoyed her meal.

Seated beside the window, she looked over the patrons laughing and talking. She felt very alone. Her eyes welled. Quickly she turned to look out the window. She stared out at the Carolina trees covered in Spanish moss without seeing them.

I don't know if I can start over again. Being alone. Eating alone. Living alone. Another failed relationship. Why does this keep happening? Why am I such a mess? She dug into her purse and pulled out a tissue. She drew in a deep, stuttered breath. *I don't think I'm strong enough to make it on my own. The pain is so deep. The pain of parting. The cold of being alone in a world of families. Another round of lost hopes and dreams. It's all too much. It's all overwhelming. What if I can't do this?*

What choice do I have? Every relationship has been a wreck. Maybe it's me. Maybe I'm not worth anything.

A wave of emotion rolled in.

No, I need to get a hold of myself. There is no choice between abuse and loneliness. I can't run anymore. There is nowhere to go. This time I must face the darkness of alone. I'll find a way. Somehow.

She wiped her eyes and focused on the beauty of the hanging moss. *Look, even the trees are crying. No, I must stop it.* She watched cars pass by trying to think of nothing. She was grateful when her meal arrived.

Once home again she spent the evening watching the sky change to dark blue as a backdrop for the stars. She listened to the fading cries of gulls and pelicans, and saw what she thought was a white ibis fly overhead.

With a deep sigh she realized she was quite exhausted – empty of the emotional turmoil and tired. The stress of the last 24 hours had taken its toll and she was glad to fall asleep quickly without getting caught in the revolving thoughts that often kept her awake.

Wednesday, June 14

She woke too early for grocery shopping. While rummaging through the kitchen, she found Cassandra had stocked it with tea and coffee. She made herself a large tea, selected one of her new books, and settled on the veranda for a couple of hours of reading.

Several pages into the book, she heard the door close next door. A tall, handsome, sandy-haired man in his mid–30s walked to a pickup in the driveway and loaded some construction gear. Based on the equipment she presumed this to be Cassandra's brother. He called back into the house and Cassandra came out to hand him a thermos. She waved him off and turned back to the house, but paused when she spotted Juleena on the veranda.

She came over to check she was happy with the accommodations and if there was anything she needed. They chatted for a couple of minutes and Juleena offered her a tea or coffee. With steaming mugs they returned to the veranda. Juleena liked her and they settled into a long conversation like old friends. They talked about their work, their family and lives.

Cassandra told about her marriage to an Internet security consultant Ryan, who was on contract in Atlanta for the next several months, and her small Internet jewellery business. Juleena told of her job and that she was on a break from men. Cass was interested to hear Juleena had spent the summers of her youth in Edisto. When she found out Peggy Morgan was her grandmother, she said, "My mom and Aunt Peggy were very good friends. She wasn't our real aunt, but we loved her like a member of our family. You must be Jules! Aunt Peggy talked about you." They compared ages and figured Juleena was two years older than Cass, and two years younger than her brother Ethan. After much discussion they decided they knew many people in common, and Jules thought it strange she didn't remember Cass or Ethan.

As Cass left she invited Juleena over that night for dinner and a girl's movie night. She explained it was midweek to accommodate the schedule of one of the ladies who regularly worked the weekend evenings. Juleena hesitated, then accepted wondering if one of the ladies might be the daughter of her grammy's neighbour. Melody, a few years older, looked after her like a big sister. She had fond memories of being included in Melody's summer adventures.

After grocery shopping she spent the rest of the day at the beach.

She went for a long walk up the coast, at least a mile, enjoying the waves washing over her feet. She laughed at the killdeers and sandpipers running in the wake. On the way back she looked carefully for her grammy's house and found it. Other than fresh paint and a new roof, it was the same bungalow on stilts. It was the last house before the start of Point Street. She remembered sleeping on the cool porch and waking to the sunrise bursting through the wall of windows.

Back then she was a girl of the tides, poking about the sand like the shorebirds looking for crabs, starfish and stranded sea cucumbers. Once she found a whalebone and brought it home. She remembered her grammy hung it above her bed for the summer. She fondly thought of this woman's generosity to care for her every summer and put value on her scavenged beach finds, only because she found them.

She stooped to pick up a beautiful pen shell. She used to scour the beaches for intact shells to sell to the local gift shop for a bit of spending money. She used to know all the names. Her favourite, and it seemed the favourite of the gift shop, were the calicos – clams and scallops. She dropped the pen shell back on the beach, wondering if collecting and selling shells was even legal anymore.

Looking at the sand dunes covered in sea grass and oats, she knew this was an ever-changing landscape, but she was not deterred from looking carefully at the dunes south of her grammy's old house. She walked slowly past several large and rather new-looking houses. Then she spotted a small, older house she recognized and she knew the weeping dune was just a bit farther south.

She carefully made her way into the taller dunes, turned and walked through the valleys. She knew it was silly to think the same dune would still be here, waiting for her return, but enjoyed the nostalgic walk anyway.

At the base of the second dune she came across three flat stones placed in a line. Smiling she wondered if another summer girl discovered this spot and felt it was her private hideaway. As she got closer she saw writing on the stones. Intrigued she leaned over to read. The first one said, "My tribute." This didn't sound like a young person.

She read the next one. "The One who paints in colour and clouds." Spoken from the heart of an artist and the soul of an observer.

Curious, she read the third one. "The One who draws out the paths for the wind to follow." She looked around for other clues to the identity of the stone writer, but the dunes would not give up their secrets.

She reread the three stones, wanting to commit the words to memory. She carefully stepped away feeling she'd intruded on someone's private thoughts and headed back out to the beach. She settled on a spot near the secret dune, set up a totable beach lounger to read and pulled out her book. She watched the waves rolling onto the beach for a long time before she began reading.

Later that afternoon she returned to the apartment to shower off the salt and sand. Ready ahead of time she picked up her phone and sat in a rattan Chesapeake chair to check for messages – only a dozen calls from Anders. She turned her phone off. She thought about the events that brought her back here. She'd forgotten how much she loved the smell and sounds of the place. A wave of contentment washed over her. *I'm home. This is my home.* The thought of finding something so precious that she hadn't known she'd lost caused her eyes to brim with tears.

With a deep sigh she blinked away the evidence of lost years.

She considered her first day on her own and opened her new journal to log her thoughts.

Wednesday, June 14

I'm done with the constant torment and I've stepped out on my own. I'm afraid of being alone. Now that I think about it, I've fled from being alone at all costs. But I've reached a crossroad – an opportunity to take my life in a different direction. I'm now more afraid of staying with Anders than being alone. Time to change roads.

I'd rather deal with the painful emptiness of being alone than face verbal assaults on my mind and physical assaults on my body. Yes. This was long overdue. I don't know why I let it go so long – so long that I no longer feel like much of a person now. I feel like I've let go of everything that is me.

In my head I know this to be a good decision, but my heart still fears being alone. I hope the weight of alone doesn't outweigh what needs to be done.

The feelings of loss and grief lurk in my thoughts waiting to ambush my determination and sink me into deep darkness. I'm afraid of the depth of the black hole awaiting me. What if there is no way out? What if I just keep falling deeper and deeper?

I can't survive another failed relationship, but I can't go back. I look at the new road and I can't see what's ahead. Staying on the Anders road looks red and painful. The crossroad looks black. What if this new road is just blackness? Can I keep going down a black road?

No. I must stop being fearful. I know there is no option. I must walk through the darkness until I see a light at the end. I must stop focusing on the negative. I need to think about the positive.

I think it's good I've returned to a place that used to bring me great comfort. What awaits me here – this place of sky, sea and sand? I'd forgotten how much I loved warm summer nights and the smell of saltwater. I feel like I've finally come home. A home I haven't known for over half my life.

I find myself at the intersection of present and past – life's junction of people, place and memories. I wait at the red light of the intersection, pausing to find myself. I hope there's enough of me still alive. And I wonder what this new path holds for me? Will I finally find happiness?

My word for today is Intersection.

Chapter 4 | Reawakening

She realized time had slipped by while writing in her new journal. It was time to head over to Cass' for ladies movie night. Although she looked forward to the companionship night, she always felt nervous around new people. She took comfort in knowing at least Cassandra and hoped she would have friends equally as friendly.

When she saw the second car pull in the driveway, she grabbed a hoodie and a cake she'd bought that morning, and headed next door. As she approached the door, one of the women opened it and invited her in. "You must be the gal next door. Glad you could join us. I'm Victoria, but everyone calls me Vicky."

"Thank you. Nice to meet you, Vicky. I'm Juleena Morgan."

Another woman heard the exchange. "Morgan? Cass mentioned you spent your summers here with your grandmother. Would that be Peggy Morgan?"

"Yes, she was my grammy. Did you know her?"

"Yes. I remember her as a gracious, kindhearted woman, like a grandma. I'm Katherine – Kit."

"She was definitely all that to me. I loved my summers here with Grammy and missed her terribly when she passed. Nice to meet you, Kit."

"If I remember, Peggy used to call you Jules?"

"Yes. I haven't heard that name in a long time. Grammy was the last person to call me that."

"When Cass mentioned you spent your summers here, I didn't recognize your name. I always thought Jules was short for Julie. Welcome to our Edisto Ladies' Dinner and a Movie night."

"Thanks, Kit. I didn't know the protocol for tonight, so I brought a cake." They headed for the kitchen. Curious, Cass opened the box. It was a cherry, whipped cream and chocolate decadent dessert which elicited much delight from the ladies.

"Juleena, you've brought our favourite cake for celebrations. So ladies, what should we celebrate tonight?"

"Jules has come back home!" said Kit.

Another woman entered the kitchen. "What's going on?"

Vicky turned and said, "Hey Maddie. Let me introduce you to Juleena – Jules Morgan – Peggy Morgan's granddaughter. She's the gal Cass mentioned. And Jules has brought our decadent celebration cake, so we are celebrating her homecoming."

Maddie shook hands with Juleena. "Welcome home, Jules. I'm Madeline or Maddie."

Jules. She liked that they all took to that nickname. She really felt welcomed, and her nervousness and hesitation gave way to embracing their friendship.

Another woman entered with a couple of boxes of pizza. Jules immediately recognized her as the chef at Grover's Bar and Grill where she had dinner the night before. Once the pizza boxes were on the counter, Jules extended her hand. "Hi, I'm Juleena Morgan – Jules. You're Chef Heather, right? We met last night at the restaurant."

Laughing, she shook her hand. "Just Heather is fine, although these ladies of nicknames often call me Heeth. Welcome to our regular dinner and a movie night."

It was quite informal. Everyone helped themselves to the food and after bowing in prayer, they sat around the coffee table, chattering over their meal.

Maddie said, "I don't know if you've heard, but Old Mac is in the hospital. Last Sunday night when his daughter was visiting, he wasn't feeling well and felt out of breath. She said he went pale grey and sweaty. She called 911 and they took him by ambulance into Charleston. It turns out he had a small heart attack."

Digging in her purse she pulled out a get well card. "I brought this from the shop. If you ladies want to sign, I'll be going into the city tomorrow and plan on stopping in to see him." Cass explained Old Mac did the accounting for all their businesses.

Heather said, "That explains why I haven't heard from him. I wanted to meet with him this week as I have some payments that need to be made right away. I hope he's going to be okay."

"The doctors said it was just a mild one. There mightn't even be any damage. So, are you going to try your hand at bookkeeping again?" Vicky said, which brought a round of laughter.

"No, I would surely turn all Mac's work into a mess. I'm not sure what I'm going to do."

Kit said, "I'm in the same boat. I need some accounting work done either this or next week at the latest. I don't think he's going to be able to leave the hospital and go right back to work. I think we are all going to need someone to help us in the interim."

Cass, winking at Jules said, "Jules is an accountant, you know." With a teasing grin she said, "Oh Jules, this could be a working vacation! How great would that be?" Everyone laughed and the conversation rolled on to other topics, but it got Jules thinking. She wondered if she could help these ladies out and perhaps extend her vacation. Maybe she could spend more time in Edisto exploring her roots while she decided what to do about Anders.

Actually, she knew what to do about Anders. In her head she knew it was over. Her heart knew it as well. She just needed some time for her heart to commit to it. She knew from the moment she moved in with him it would be his way, always. She thought she could make herself happy on his path. She thought companionship was worth giving up herself.

Then it dawned on her. Since her grammy's death she'd done everything necessary to not be alone. For many years her family consisted solely of a father who had no time for her. As a result she clung to any male who paid her attention even if it put her mental health at risk.

Yes, this place is good for me. Maybe I could work out the details with my boss to spend the summer here. Maybe I could regain the happiness, courage and strength I used to have.

When the conversation hit a lull, she said, "If you guys are serious about needing some accounting work done, I'd be glad to help until Mac gets on his feet again. I'm considering extending my vacation for the whole summer. I just need to work it out with my employer and the woman I'm renting from here." Cass laughed and said there was a room if she wanted. "I work on accounting implementation projects and I'm between projects right now, so it might work out for everyone, if you are interested."

Heather was the first to answer. "I don't know about the others, but I'm abysmal with accounting and would be very grateful for your help. I would gladly pay you what I pay Mac. He has us all on a cloud-based application, so it would be easy to get you set up. Mac normally picks up my paperwork, then works from home, but you could come to the restaurant and work on my computer in the office, if you don't have yours with you. That way I'm available if you have questions."

Before Jules could answer, Kit said, "Same for me. I'm terrible at staying on top of the accounting. I have a business selling glass art to specialty shops, jewellery makers, and I sell glass trinkets online as well as custom-made works. I'm an artist, not a bookkeeper. I know this wouldn't be as exciting as the projects you normally work with, but I would appreciate your help as well."

Maddie said, "I'm going to need help at month end too. I own the gift shop in town and have a substantial amount of work every couple of weeks. At least it's substantial if I have to do it. Mac seems to get things in order in less than a day. If you're offering, I'm happily jumping in too."

28

Vicky said, "Oh Jules, this is very generous of you. I suspect all of Mac's clients are going to be scrambling at month end. And I know everyone would be happy to pay you to keep us going. I own a funeral home off island, but I could meet you at my home here in Edisto Beach, if that would work for you."

Cass said, "Looks like it's unanimous. While I have a small jewellery business, my husband and I have his consulting work along with several of his monitoring and maintenance contracts that are on monthly billing. Neither of us likes or wants to get into the accounting, so we definitely need help as well."

Laughing, Jules said, "Okay, it's a deal at least for the month and longer if I can make the arrangements and if you still need help. If we could do mornings, then I would have my afternoons for vacation time. And whatever Mac charges is fine by me. Let me give you my email and we can follow up with arrangements. I have no particular vacation plans, so I'm pretty flexible." Heather asked if tomorrow would be too soon. Jules laughed and agreed to come by in the morning.

After dessert came the big decision. What movie would they watch? It was chick flick night and was a choice between two recent releases. They let Jules make the final decision as they were celebrating her homecoming and she was the favoured guest because of her offer to help.

As they were cleaning up the kitchen and getting ready to start the movie, Ethan came in. "Women of Edisto! So what movie have you chosen tonight?"

Cass said, "Hey Ethan, I didn't hear you drive up. You remember me telling you about Juleena? You might remember her as Jules Morgan. She's Peggy Morgan's granddaughter."

"I remember a skinny little kid always on the beach."

"That was me, alright. I was collecting shells. I needed money to spend on candy and bubblegum."

"Old Man Harvey was pretty generous with the townie kids. He paid us well for those shells. Glad you got in on the deal. Ooh, is that a celebration cake?"

Cass laughed at her brother. "Yes, Jules brought it and we decided to celebrate her homecoming. And yes, you can help yourself."

He cleaned up the leftover pizza and cut a big slice of the cake. He headed for the back deck and said, "Enjoy your movie!"

Cass turned off the lights and closed the shutters to darken the room, and they all settled in to enjoy the movie. Jules expected quite a bit of chatter through the movie, thinking it inevitable with a group of women, but was pleasantly surprised that they were pretty quiet – except for Maddie. She took some ribbing for crying.

It's been a very long time since she had friends that were her own. She happened upon a wonderful group of accomplished women. Who knew that in a small sleepy vacation town there would be such a collection of successful businesswomen, and they were all good people. She hoped she could work out an extended time here and forge a good friendship with them.

Wednesday, June 14

All around me is peace and warmth, yet inside I remain in chaos. The commitment to walking another path brings new fears. I now live with the turmoil of confronting myself and confronting change. Sometimes I look ahead and see hope and beauty, but then I think my intersection is really a choice of living alone or living unloved.

It's like the Neil Diamond song "I am...I said." It's really hard to face the truth of the pain of loneliness expressed. The line about a desperate emptiness that won't release him just crushes me. The words and music capture my ache and longing not to face life alone. Aloneness isn't just the physical absence of others. It has a voice that speaks directly to the heart. My eyes see people everywhere, yet I only see black-ness inside. Ears hear laughter and love all around, but my internal being only hears the resounding echo of loneliness. Today I saw the sun, felt its warmth on my skin. I saw the unceasing waves bubbling and heard their gurgling laughter. Yet my soul doesn't match the life around me. I fear walking through life alone. I fear the emptiness, the blackness. The overwhelming silence of alone.

And yet, if I'm honest, I've been alone most of my life.

When with Anders I remained alone. At parties, at home, even when he held me in his arms, I felt I was an obligation. What is wrong with me that he could never find room in his heart for me? I never felt he loved me. My heart can no longer take the pain of his lack of love for anyone but him-self. And I don't want to take the next step down to physical abuse in hopes he will love me.

With the men before him, I was a convenience, a social ne-cessity, a conquest, but never a loved and cherished treasure. Maybe that kind of love is a fairy tale. Or maybe I'm not worthy of that kind of love.

And then there's Dad. I never had one kindness from his mouth or hand. I longed for him to love me, but he re-mained cold and uncaring. He did the bare minimum. I was his only child. Was I not worth more?

What makes me so worthless? Why does no one love or care about me? Can I stand alone? I hope so.

I have a choice. Return to a loveless relationship and suffer feelings of worthlessness or walk alone and suffer loneliness. Neither path offers anything but pain. I've tried the one path and intimately know the pain. Perhaps it is time to walk the other path. It can't be any worse, and perhaps it will be slightly better in time when my wounds heal.

Now I see the path of worthlessness led to painful loneliness. And that took me to a dark valley of desperation – I became one of those clingy females even I don't like. But still I found nothing to fill my hollowness. I've tried to put all my pain to sleep. I thought anyone was better than no one. Another person would be a distraction from the emptiness. Yes, at first my days were hopeful and my nights warm. But as the newness passed, I found hope faded. Yet I clung to an empty promise of love.

I have no strength left to cling to a false hope.

But then Edisto! Jules, the skinny beach kid, has returned home. There is a little piece of the long-lost me that's slowly awakening again. The girl who had childhood friends – I can actually have friends of my own. Maybe I'm not really Juleena who let her heart become anesthetized. Maybe I'm Jules and I'm back. The real me is awakening to a new life.

I'm scared I can't do this on my own. I'm not sure I believe enough in myself. Well really, I'm not sure there's enough left to believe in. But the alternative of the last several years is not an option anymore. It just can't be.

I sense something so much better. And I miss the girl on the beach who was me.

Jules. I think I might like her. Maybe she is the strong person in me.

Changing my word for today to Reawakening.

Chapter 5 | Reconnection

Thursday, June 15

The next morning before heading to Grover's Bar and Grill to get started on Heather's books, she called her boss. After briefly explaining she wanted to take time to reconnect with her family roots, they agreed she would take the remainder of the summer as unpaid leave. She knew she would be bringing in some money from the various bookkeeping jobs here and felt very comfortable not collecting her regular pay. Since there were no projects on the near horizon, a summer vacation worked well for both of them.

She spent the next few hours with Heather getting familiar with the way Mac set up her books, and managed to complete about three-quarters of the work. With the books up to date and the bulk of cheques prepared to go out, Heather was quite pleased with the progress. They made arrangements for Jules to return the next morning to finish off the work.

She returned home, changed, collected her book and lounger, and headed down to the beach. Once there she decided on the same spot as the previous day. As she settled in she thought about her first days at Edisto Beach. She replayed her evening with her new friends, her temporary job and the full summer that stretched out before her.

Looking out at the steady waves rolling in, hearing their rhythmic crash on the shore and feeling the steady warm breeze on her skin, she opened her heart to the moment. *I've missed this place. For the briefest of time I get to forget my world and feel wrapped in a comfortable everything-is-right-in-my-universe cocoon.* She closed her eyes, relishing her affection and connection with this small town.

She got to thinking about her discovery of the secret dune hideaway and tried to recall the words written on the stones. It was something about clouds, sunsets and wind. It was worded with more artistic flair, but she couldn't quite remember.

Her desire to read those words overwhelmed her thoughts and she headed for the dunes. She wondered who wrote such beautiful things and why they would leave them out in the dunes. They really captured what she felt about the place.

As she approached the valley of the dune, she was surprised to see a fourth stone. Whoever the author was, they hadn't finished writing. She bent down to read the new one. "The One who created the ocean as a mirror reflecting the mood of the day."

She thought about that for a moment. *It's true. Sometimes the ocean is turquoise blue reflecting a bright and happy sunny day. But it becomes a dark steel grey on an introspective rainy day. The ocean is a mood mirror. I really like this author! Who could it be? I wonder if I will ever know?*

She then reread all the stones in order. It wasn't clouds and sunsets. It said, "paints in colours and clouds." She imagined sunsets. She loved that line. She rehearsed the lines several times so she wouldn't forget them.

Once back on the beach, she considered asking Cass if she knew anything about it, but then thought better of it. To do so would be a betrayal of the author. Granted, they left the stones out where they could be found, tucked in-between the dunes and hidden from the public view. *No, I'll keep this discovery to myself.*

When she got home she wrote out the words on a sheet of paper, folded and tucked it into her book as a bookmark. She prepared a cold chicken and salad dinner from the store-bought supplies, and sat on the front veranda to eat and enjoy the gradual onset of night.

Cass came out looking up and down the street. She noticed Jules and waved as she headed over. "I hear you are a marvel with accounting. Heeth mentioned you were in this morning and completed most of her work in one morning."

Laughing, Jules said, "No, not a marvel! I've used that software before, so it was pretty easy to find my way around and get the work done. I'm popping by briefly tomorrow to finish up."

"Have the other ladies booked up your mornings next week, or do you have time to fit me in?"

"I'm out at Kit's on Monday, Vicky's on Wednesday and Maddie's on Thursday and probably Friday as well. So, Tuesday?"

"Tuesday's perfect! Thanks, Jules, for helping us all out. Oh, are you busy Saturday evening? All the churches on the island put on a beach barbeque and get-together for all the islanders. You are welcome to join us. Several of Mac's clients have been asking about you and it'd be a great chance to meet everyone. Ethan and I will be heading down around 6:30, if you'd like to come with us."

"Okay, thanks! Do I need to bring anything?"

"No. The churches provide everything. Just bring a jacket for the evening. It generally goes well into the night for those without small children. And I'm glad you're coming. Oh, I spoke with Mac's daughter today. She thinks he'll be released by Sunday, but will spend a week or two with her before coming home. She mentioned to him that you're helping us all out until he's on his feet again. She said that made a big difference to him. He was pushing to come home and get back to work because he was concerned for us. He was very relieved to know there is no rush. So she asked if I would offer you her thanks as well."

"I'm glad to hear he's doing well. I appreciate that you made sure he understood I'm not stealing his clients from him, just helping out. I wouldn't want him worried about his business."

"I think he only agreed to spending a few weeks with his daughter because you're taking care of things. So I think you've taken away his worry, not added to it. I was just heading down to the beach for a walk. Care to join me? I'd love the company."

"Okay, let me take in my dishes and get my shoes."

They headed down the street, talking and laughing when Ethan drove up from behind and stopped beside them. He leaned out of the window to talk. "Sorry I'm later than I expected, but I got all the drywall up and all the joints done."

"No worries. I've already eaten and your dinner's in the fridge."

"Okay, thanks. Are you going for a walk down on the beach? Mind if I join you? Or is it strictly ladies only?"

Looking at Jules Cass said, "I doubt we'll talk about anything you shouldn't hear. Park the truck and we'll wait for you."

He gave a quick look at Jules to be sure she was okay, then threw the truck in reverse to park in their driveway. He jogged down to catch up with them.

"Thanks for waiting. Since I've moved back I try to get to the beach every day after work. It doesn't always work out, but I'm glad to have two beautiful women with me today. It enhances my reputation."

Jules looked at him with a smile and raised eyebrows. Cass leaned forward to look at him past Jules. "You've got that right, buddy. We're the only reason you look good. You have no Casanova reputation on your own."

He blew her a kiss and they laughed. The conversation wandered from how Jules was enjoying Edisto to the expected weather for the barbeque. Jules asked Ethan what brought him back and if he planned on staying awhile.

After a pause he said, "Well, that is a story."

Looking at him Jules sensed she'd hit tender territory. He walked a little slower and his head was bent down. "Hey, if it's none of my business, that's okay."

"No, no. It's not that." Lifting his head he patted her shoulder.

"I'm still sorting out my thoughts. I'm kind of at loose ends."

With a deep sigh he said, "After high school I wandered around Australia and New Zealand for several years eventually picking up odd jobs. I then studied to be a minister in Tennessee. When I'd finished, I married and started working in a church in Virginia. We then moved to Louisiana for a couple years, and then Texas. I kept pressing to start a family, but Gabriel kept putting me off. By the time we got to Texas, I sensed there were problems, but put it out of my mind.

"Then sitting in a restaurant one day, I saw Gabriel with another man. It was clear they were in a relationship. I confronted her that evening and she admitted she no longer loved me and wanted out of our marriage. She left that night and I haven't seen her since.

"The church was very supportive – maybe a bit too much. It began to feel like pity. I questioned my continued role there for several months. Then came the day I was served with divorce papers. With my signature on the divorce, I resigned from the church. I just wasn't sure what I wanted from life. I've come home to figure myself out and figure out what God would have me do.

"I've been here for six months now. This place has a wonderful way of healing hurting hearts and washing away the burdens of the soul. Now I'm waiting for my next open door and in the meantime I'm enjoying being back on the water."

"I'm sorry to hear of your divorce. A broken relationship isn't easy. Are you thinking of going back to church work?"

"I don't know. I don't think so. I like to think God will bring something great out of this tragedy, but I've not been informed yet what that great thing is." Looking out over the water, he said, "Listen, enough of me. What about you? Cass tells me you plan on staying for the summer."

With a fleeting smile she said, "Yes. It seems I'm here to find myself as well." Hesitating for a moment she said, "I was in a relationship I should not have been in. He was mentally abusive, but when he swung his fist and missed, he crossed my line and I decided to leave. We were on the first day of our vacation. So I grabbed my things and slipped away, taking one of the first flights out which happened to be to Charleston. Once I heard Charleston I knew I wanted to come here. I remember so many good times here with my grammy."

"Peggy was a good friend of our mom. I remember her well. She and Mom used to make Thanksgiving and Christmas dinners together. The meals were fantastic. I had to wear eating pants to make it through the meal."

"Eating pants?"

Cass jumped in. "Ethan makes it sound like something special. It's just sweat pants. Mom would complain about him wearing sweats, so at the tender age of 12 he took to calling them eating pants. It made Auntie Peggy laugh so hard, they let him wear them to every holiday meal after that. Now he calls it tradition and still wears sweats."

"Not only is it tradition, it's now a trend. All the guys who have any eating self-respect wear eating pants."

Cass reached across and pushed him into the surf. Laughing, he kicked water at her, catching both Cass and Jules. A water fight broke out between the three of them worthy of 12-year-olds. Clearly defeated by the overwhelming forces of the women, he gave up and fell in the water. Jules offered her hand to pull him up, but he pulled her in and a full-blown splash fight erupted.

They finally headed for the shore, soaking wet from head to toe and laughing. The conversation took a lighter turn and they enjoyed each other's company like three best friends on their first day of summer holidays.

On the way back up their street, Ethan said, "I talked with Matt last night. He called to see if we could get together Saturday night for dinner. I didn't realize he was coming and had booked time in the rental with you."

"Yes, he called a few weeks ago on the spur of the moment. I'm sorry. I thought I told you. It must have been Ryan I told. Anyway, he mentioned he sold his latest app for a healthy profit and wants to take a break before tackling his next endeavour. He's booked in for the summer. He wanted to get in touch with you, so I gave him your cell number. Did you invite him to the beach party? I hope you're still coming."

"Yes, I'm still coming and yes, I invited him."

Cass turned to Jules. "He's our cousin. Before we were born my dad's brother bought a sugar cane plantation in Barbados. One year when we were quite young, he came for a visit at Christmas with a young lad he had adopted. Matt's dad was the plantation manager for our uncle. Both of Matt's parents died in suspicious circumstances. Our aunt and uncle took him into their home and over time got through the paperwork necessary to adopt him. Although he's of Irish heritage, his family was considered Barbadian, or as Matt prefers, Bajan. His ancestors moved to Barbados over a century ago. He's an interesting mix of Irish and Islander – and we all love him. It'll be fun to have him around for a few months."

They were back home, and Jules said good evening and went in to change out of her ocean-soaked clothes and shower off the salt and sand. That evening she settled into bed, thinking about her day. She smiled at the playful fun she had with her two new friends. It sure felt good to not worry about saying the wrong thing and being on the receiving end of a tirade of insults. She thought briefly about the stark difference in her life with Anders and the short couple of days back at Edisto, and realized how far she'd allowed her life to slip into unhappiness.

Thursday, June 15

I'm comfortable here. I feel connected here. I like that Cass invited me for a walk and Ethan wanted to join us. I feel like they actually want to include me. Ethan said something about the healing power of Edisto on hurting hearts and minds. Well, he said it more eloquently.

It's been a very long time since I laughed with friends. My heart is still smiling. I can't believe we let loose with child-like abandon and played like little kids. And the joy wasn't squashed with insults and humiliation. Just joy. A happy heart and mind. Yes, there is healing here for me.

Why haven't I ever encountered people like this in New York City?

I feel drawn to this place. The people are welcoming, warm, friendly and fun. I'm meeting my real self – no, not meeting myself. I'm reconnecting with myself. Reconnecting with Edisto. Reconnecting with my roots.

I am happier as Jules. I don't wish to live as Juleena ever again. I think I can make it on this other path. Just maybe.

My word for today is reconnection.

Chapter 6 | Heartache

Friday, June 16

The next morning, she finished the accounting work for Heather by printing all the payroll cheques and left them on her desk awaiting her signature. Before heading home and to the beach, she stopped at the grocery store to pick up supplies for the weekend. She planned on spending the afternoon on the beach reading.

By midafternoon the offshore breeze had kicked up. There were a number of surfers enjoying the waves, but wind picked up the sand from the dune tops and blew it into anyone sitting on the beach. It felt like sitting in front of a sandblaster.

She decided to abandon the reading and went for a walk. As she passed the secret dune she couldn't resist checking to see if a new stone had appeared. There was nothing new.

She stood for awhile listening. She wondered if the memory of her youth of a weeping dune was just something she imagined. *Was it even possible for a dune to weep? Well no, not actually weep, but to make the sound of weeping?*

Without drawing a conclusion she returned to the beach to watch the surfers. Despite the wind the day was warm and she stepped into the foaming water. She loved the feel of its ebb and flow. The receding wave suctioned away the sand around her feet, then washed it back over. She wiggled her toes, letting her feet sink deeper into the sand.

After enjoying the churning surf, she headed deeper to play in the waves and renew her bodysurfing skills. When tired she headed home to clean out the sand collected in her bathing suit and hair, and read on the veranda. Ethan came home early that evening and waved a warm hello. "Just heading down the beach."

"It's quite windy today."

"That's okay. I won't mind letting the wind blow out the dark bits of my soul. See you later."

A few minutes later a Mercedes pulled up. A tall silver-haired, blue eyed man in his late 20s – too young for silver hair – got out and looked up at the veranda. Spotting Jules he said, "Hello."

She responded. He nodded and opened the back door, retrieved a bag from the backseat, then headed next door to Cass'. When he got to the door, Jules could hear an excited greeting and presumed this must be Cousin Matthew.

Almost an hour later she saw Ethan coming back from the beach. A Porsche pulled into the driveway and Ethan jogged up to open the driver door. "Hey Matthew! Long time, no see. How are you?" A tall, extremely well-cut, bronzed man got out of the car and briefly stretched. They hugged and patted each other on the back.

If this is Matthew, who was the other guy? I wonder if he's Cass' husband.

"Come on in and say hello to Cass. Actually, it looks like Ryan's home too. It'll be like a family reunion."

A large blue heron flew overhead, distracting Jules and by the time it disappeared behind the treetops, the driveway was empty. In half an hour another car pulled up and the driver delivered a couple of pizzas.

Jules smiled and silently wished Cass and Ethan a happy family evening. Then a heaviness washed over her – the pain of her long-standing loneliness. She hadn't felt the love and warmth of family since her grammy was alive, and she became acutely aware of a gigantic hole in her life. Feeling restless, she decided to take a walk and headed in the opposite direction of the windy beach. She wandered along the residential streets, looking at the different homes and wondering what all the people did for a living that allowed them to live in a vacation town.

After a couple of hours and well after the sun set, she headed back home. She intentionally did not look toward Cass' house. She didn't want the wounds to open up again. Rather than read on the veranda, she stayed in. At the approach of midnight, she climbed into bed.

Friday, June 16

A family reunion. Oh, what pain to watch people who belong to family reunite. I remain without family.

I saw the love these people have for each other and the joy in seeing each other. My heart aches. It rips my soul open. The pain is deep and wants to swallow me, to drown me in its depths of loneliness. Empty. Dark. Cold. Alone. And body aching pain. I'm being sucked back into that dark valley of lonely desperation.

Oh, I can't stay in heartache. In a weak moment, I'm liable to run back to the lesser pain of Anders or some other man. Oh but that is a lie. The pain of worthlessness with Anders is ongoing, opening new wounds daily. I hope this heartache will recede in time. Still, this pain is crushing. It may be too much for me and it might be easier to go back to Anders – oh, I don't want to do that. I must find strength and rise above this.

43

How can I be so normal at work, then be a simpering, clingy woman in my personal life? Maybe I could shut down my emotions. Focus on work. Work will be what I'm about. But no, that was the path of my coldhearted father. It is not for me.

No. I must get a grip on my heartache. I cannot let this continue. I need to find a way to be me and not fall for the first man that comes along who seems interested. I can now see I've never found in the arms of another a balm for the desolation I feel. What is the answer? Does everyone feel this way? I just don't see the hollow emptiness in the eyes of Cass and Ethan. There must be something more than living with this heartache or killing my emotions forever.

I have to find what these people have. I cannot stay with this heartache. In this condition I would end up throwing my heart away yet again. And be back in the same place I am today.

My word for today is a phrase: I'm done with heartache.

Chapter 7 | Starvation

Saturday, June 17

She got up late the next morning, made a hot tea, grabbed a banana and yogurt, and headed for the veranda. A few minutes later the door at the far end of the veranda opened and the tanned, dark-brown-haired man appeared in shorts, a rumpled T-shirt, carrying a cup of coffee. Stealing a look at him, she thought of Anders – too good-looking for his own good. After a few sips he noticed her and came over. "Hello. Looks like we will be sharing our veranda for the next couple of months. I'm Matthew Thomas."

"Hi Matthew. You must be Cass and Ethan's cousin. I'm Jules Morgan. I hear from Ethan you're here for the summer?" She noted he hadn't shaved yet and looked like a rumpled boy just out of bed.

"Yes. I'm between gigs and I thought I'd spend the summer here sorting out what my next development effort will be. How about you? I hear you're here for the summer too?"

"Yes. I'm taking the summer to reconnect with my roots. I used to spend my summers here with my grammy when I was young."

"That's right. You're the granddaughter of Auntie Peggy. I loved her. She was such a warm, loving woman. So, what do you do for a living?"

"I'm an accountant and work for a consulting firm. We help companies implement new accounting systems. And I'm between projects too. For the summer, I'm helping out several businesswomen in town with their bookkeeping while their accountant recovers from a heart attack."

"Old Mac had a heart attack? Is he okay?"

"I hear it was only mild and he's coming home this weekend. Well, he'll be staying with his daughter for a week or two, then coming home."

He thought for a long moment. "Huh, you're Peggy Morgan's granddaughter – and you're covering for Old Mac? Interesting. Small world."

Before she could ask what he meant, Ethan joined them on the veranda.

"Hey Jules. I came looking for you last evening. We ordered in pizza and I came to invite you to join us. Ryan came home for the weekend and Cass was bragging about your accounting talents. I see you've met Matt."

"Yes, thanks. Sorry we missed each other last night. I felt like a walk and wandered around the neighbourhood a bit."

With a raised eyebrow and a smile he said, "Oh, looking to move here permanently?"

That caught Jules off guard and she stumbled for an answer.

"I'm just teasing," he said.

Moving over to Matt he patted him on the back and said, "Good morning, bud. Feel up for a game of golf? If we leave now, we can make the one open tee time."

"Sounds good. Give me five minutes," and he disappeared into his room.

Leaning on the deck rail, Ethan turned back to Jules and said, "Any plans for today?"

"If the wind has died down, I thought I'd spend time at the beach. I had fun yesterday bodysurfing, and I love reading while listening to the wind and waves. And then Cass invited me to join you this evening for the beach barbeque."

"I checked the weather for today and it looks like it shouldn't be too windy at all. You'll have a good day and it should be a perfect night for a beach party. I see you read a lot. What kind of books are you into?"

Turning her book over she said, "Probably not what you'd expect for a woman. I like adventure, spy and detective stories, and well written drama."

"Have you read any books by Clive Cussler or Brad Thor? They are a bit like Tom Clancy."

"Yes, I've read a few of Cussler's books, but not Brad Thor. And I like Tom Clancy too."

"Brad Thor is quite good. I've got the entire Scot Harvath series. I can drop them off if you would like to borrow them."

"Okay. Now that I'm staying for the summer, I'll need more reading material."

Matt came out with a fresh T-shirt on and combed hair. "Want to take the Porsche?"

"Hmm, my truck or the Porsche. Like choosing between an elephant and a thoroughbred. Tough decision."

Matt tossed his keys to Ethan.

Turning back to Jules Ethan said, "I'll drop the books off by tomorrow. Keep them as long as you need."

And off the men went to pick up Ethan's clubs and head out to the Plantation Course beside Grover's Bar and Grill.

Jules headed down to the beach, packed up for a day of bodysurfing, and reading and napping on an inflatable float beyond the breaking waves. Once settled she headed for the secret dune. As she approached she saw a fifth stone. She picked up the pace, eager to read the new thought. "The One who motivates the sea to dance and sing."

She felt the joy of the writer, almost like it was too abundant and overflowing. *Maybe that's why they're writing these – out of a heart that is too full and needs to let a little out. I could use a good dose of that kind of happy.*

When home, she opened her book to the folded piece of paper and added this new line to the ones she wrote earlier.

She'd showered and planned to read on the veranda for half an hour until 6:30 when the folks next door would be heading down to the beach for the barbeque. Matt came out of his apartment and saw her. "Hey Jules. I was hoping to catch you out here. Cass has invited both of us over for drinks before we head down to the beach. I'm heading next door now. Care to join me?"

"Okay. That sounds great. Let me get my sweater for later."

As she locked up she said, "Have you been to one of these barbeques before?"

"Oh, quite a few, I guess. They're pretty fun. Good Carolina food and drink, good people, dancing, beach fires and all the s'mores you can eat."

"Does the whole town usually come out?"

"Yes. It's normally a big crowd as a lot of the vacationers come as well. It thins out as the evening progresses, but yes, most attend. They hold a couple more later in the season as well. It's always been a pretty close-knit community."

As they neared the door, Jules said, "How was golfing this morning?"

Laughing, he said, "I'm afraid I'm a bit out of practise. Ethan won by a mile."

Matt held the door for her, guiding her in with a light hand on her back and followed her in, announcing, "Hey cousins! I've brought Jules with me!"

"In here. Are you talking about your pathetic golf game? Hey Jules. Did he tell you the truth?"

"He did. I sense a long history of golf rivalry."

Matt said, "Well, Ethan thinks he's the next Arnold Palmer, but plays like a three-par duffer."

"Hey, hey. Who beat who today?"

Cass interrupted the verbal jousting. "Okay, boys. You have all summer to sort out who is the next golf pro. Ethan, can you get Jules a drink?"

Leading Jules to the living room, Cass said, "I'd like you to meet my husband Ryan. He came in last night for the weekend. The sneak didn't tell me he was coming, did you, my love?"

"No. I thought surprises like this are good for a marriage." Holding out his hand to Jules, he said, "Nice to meet you, Jules. I've heard you will be helping us with our bookkeeping while Mac recovers. I'd like to thank you. I hate accounting and respect those who actually enjoy the work."

"Good to meet you too. I'm glad to help. I think I'm here on Tuesday to sort you out. And I greatly respect those who actually enjoy sorting out computers and networks."

Ethan came in with a glass of white wine for her. "Word around the island is everyone is lining up to meet you tonight and get some of your time to take care of their books."

Laughing, she said, "I doubt everyone actually needs a bookkeeper, but I'm sure I can help out whoever needs it."

Ryan said, "Hmm, I think you'll be quite popular tonight."

They chatted about Matthew's app sale, Ryan's current project and the renovations Ethan was doing on his newly purchased home. At 6:30 as everyone started for the door, Jules looked for her sweater.

"Looking for this?" Ethan said, picking it up from a chair in the kitchen.

"Yes, thanks. I don't know if I'll need it tonight, but thought I should bring it along should it cool down."

"No worries. I'll keep my eye on it in case it tries to slip away again."

Once outside Ethan stopped to pick up a couple of folding chairs. The others were already walking a bit ahead. Ryan turned back and looked Ethan up and down. "Hey Ethan, I thought you'd be in eating pants tonight."

Matt turned around and walking backwards said, "Eating pants! I haven't thought about eating pants in a long time!"

"Hey, hey, now. Eating pants are both trendy and traditional."

"Oh, right. GQ features them every issue."

"You just wish you could carry them off as good as me."

Turning back forward Matt called over his shoulder, "You are a trendy legend in your own mind, bud!"

Ethan dropped the chairs, ran up behind Matt and faked a chokehold. "Don't be mocking the eating pants." That elicited quite a bit of laughter.

Now walking at the back and alone, Jules picked up the chairs. She watched the group interacting and thought, *they are like brothers – they know each other so well and are comfortable to tease and rough-house.* She wished she had siblings who knew her inside out and still loved her like these people. Cass was a very lucky woman.

Ethan dropped back to take the chairs back and keep her company. "Matt and Ryan have been friends since their teens. That's how Cass and Ryan met. We've been friends for a long time. Its great having the summer together again."

Quiet for a moment Jules finally said, "You're very lucky, Ethan. I envy you all for your tight family relationships."

Ethan looked at her closely, then wrapped his arm around her shoulders. "You're home now. Back with people who know you. You can be an honourary member of our family. Your grandmother was."

They looked at each other for a moment. Ethan nodded slightly and Jules smiled. "Thank you, Ethan. I might just take you up on that offer." They walked the remaining way to the beach with his arm around her.

Once on the beach some of the men were working to take several barbeques off the back of a truck. The three men went to help. Cass waited for Jules to catch up and led her to a group of ladies setting up the tables. One of the older women looked vaguely familiar.

"Mom, let me introduce you to Jules Morgan. Jules, this is my mom Sandra Thomas."

"Oh Jules, good to see you again. I remember when you were a wee one growing up."

"Good to meet you too, Mrs. Thomas. I recognized you right away. I remember you and Grammy visiting."

"Please, call me Sandra. Cass tells me you're here for the summer."

"Yes, I've made arrangements to stay until September. I'm renting one of Cass' new units."

"I hope to see more of you, then. We always considered Peggy part of our family and I'd like to think you would fill that hole for us. Oh, Greg?" She called over a tall, distinguished, grey-haired man. "Greg, do you remember Peggy Morgan's granddaughter Jules?"

Looking at her he said, "Jules!" He reached out and shook her hand warmly. "Yes, I do. You were a cute little girl growing up and I thought you would turn all the boys' heads. Welcome back to Edisto. When was your last summer?"

"Thank you. My last summer with Grammy was when I turned 14. Then the following year Dad and I returned to settle her estate and sell the property. That was a sad year for me and I've missed this place ever since. I have fond memories of my time here."

"That's right. I remember that year. We all miss Peggy. She was a wonderful woman. How long are you here for?"

"I'm here for the summer."

"I hear you're helping out with some accounting while Mac recovers. Could I book some of your time? I own the marina here in town."

"I'd be glad to help. I'm only working mornings and am booked every day this coming week. Would sometime the following week work?"

"How about Tuesday?"

"Tuesday it is."

"Say, we're taking the kids for a sail next Saturday. We're going to head south along the coast for the afternoon, have dinner onboard, then sail back. Would you like to join us?"

Cass overheard the conversation. "Dad still calls us kids. And yes, Jules, please come. I'd love a female friend among all the lads," nodding toward Ryan, Matt and Ethan.

"Okay. Thank you, Mr. Thomas."

"None of this "Mr. Thomas" stuff. Greg will do. Good. We will leave the marina at noon."

"Can I bring anything?"

"Oh, I leave the food to my wife. Sandy? Jules is going to join us next Saturday for our family sail. She's asking if there's anything she can bring."

After a bit of discussion, they decided she could bring dessert.

Kit came over and welcomed Jules. "I was hoping to run into you here. I have some people that would like to meet you." They walked a little farther down the beach to another group of people. "Randy, Doug? Let me introduce you to Jules, the accounting genius."

They both said they were glad to meet her, had heard about her helping out folks and asked if she had some time for them as well. A couple of other people overheard the conversation and introduced her to several other people. She gave out her email address to all interested and said she'd be happy to help them out in the interim. Ryan wasn't joking when he said there was a lineup of people – so many, the names were just a blur.

The organizers set up a sound system. One of the ministers got on the microphone, greeted everyone, welcomed the visitors and encouraged everyone to enjoy a good evening together. He then turned up the volume and started the music. It was their traditional opening song, "Sweet Caroline," which everyone sang as "Sweet Carolina." The locals knew all the words and sang out at their loudest volume drowning out the sound system. People danced with whoever was nearby. On the chorus the dancing paused for everyone to belt out the words.

As soon as the music started, Ethan came over to Jules, held her one hand and wrapped his other arm around her back, singing most sincerely to her. On the chorus all the couples gathered as a group, arms around each other's shoulders, swayed to the rhythm and belted out the words. *This is awesome. I have never known such a community of people that really enjoys having fun together like this. I shouldn't have been away so long.*

On the second verse he took her in his arms to dance again and continued to sing to her. Again on the final rounds of the chorus, he joined a larger group in imitating rock stars singing. There was quite a bit of air guitar, piano and horn. She couldn't help but laugh and join in.

After the first song, they turned down the volume so people could resume their conversations. As she thought about dancing with Ethan, she felt flattered and a little swept off her feet to have him pay her such attention, but as she watched him afterward, she noticed he was warm and friendly with everyone, not just her. *Maybe it's a good thing there's nothing to his attention.* He's certainly a good man and part of a great family, but she didn't feel ready for a close relationship and didn't want to put in jeopardy her friendship with any of them. She knew how these relationships always ended. Despite her heartache she needed to hold steady. She couldn't afford to fall for anyone. Best she stay strong.

She ran into Vicky and Maddie who introduced her to their husbands. Maddie's husband was the minister of the Baptist church, and the one who greeted the crowd and started the music. She was amused to see all the ministers hanging out together, laughing and talking. This was a community that truly loved and cared for each other. She had attended church with her grammy and counted herself a Christian, but had never seen true Christianity expressed so vividly. Sure, these Christian ministers had differences in opinion and doctrine, but they set those aside to love one another as commanded in the Bible.

Later in the evening she took a break from the crowds and walked away from the light of the fires to sit alone, hidden in the darkness. She wanted to watch the people from a distance and think. She looked out over the ocean. The sky over the water was dark. The first of the stars could be seen.

On reflection she knew she'd not been living a Christian life. She looked back to the townspeople and spotted Cass, Ryan and Ethan in the light of the fires. These people lived their beliefs. They loved each other unconditionally and welcomed her into their lives.

Tears filled her eyes. She blinked and looked back to the dark ocean. That is where she felt she existed. Lost and in the dark. She keenly felt the emptiness of her life. The ache squeezed her heart. She had been slowly starving for something real and meaningful. She sat desolate – alone. The light seems so bright when you've been in the darkness too long. A hot tear spilled out and rolled down her cheek. She pulled down her sweatshirt sleeve and wiped away her tears.

"Hey you. Everything okay?"

Startled, she looked back to see Matt approaching. "Yes. It's been a long time since I've been around such warmth. While it's great, it's also a bit overwhelming. I just wanted to step away and watch for awhile."

"Mind if I join you?"

"No, not at all."

He sat down beside her and they sat quietly for a moment, listening to the waves break on the shore. "I think I know what you're feeling. I first came here as an adopted kid. I had such loss in my life. I love my adopted parents dearly, but they aren't Christians like Sandra and Greg. There's just something different about this family and I finally came to the conclusion it was that they lived their Christian beliefs. They taught Ethan and Cass to live that way as well.

"For a long time I felt like I didn't deserve to be a part of their family circle. Oh, I loved being welcomed, loved and cared for, but I held myself at a distance in case it wasn't real. Then I feared it might be withdrawn, making the loneliness even more bitter. It was several years before they won me over completely.

"They are all they appear to be, Jules. It's why I keep coming back. I get filled up with the joy of Christian family life, then return to my life only for it to slowly dissipate. Until this past year I'd not found a gal that would help me form that kind of family for myself. So I'm back for another fill-up of family."

"My grammy was like Greg and Sandra. I once had this in my life when I was young. Well, at least for the summers. Grammy died when

I was 14 and I lost all connection with Edisto, and all sense of family. There was just my dad and me, and he was not all that interested in me.

"I didn't realize what a huge hole had grown inside me over the years. This week I've slowly come to see the chasm. I've been emotionally starving for a long time and need to take in happiness and friendship in manageable bites. The awareness of all I've missed has hit me like a deep wound. I think I just need time to process things in my head. I don't know why I'm telling you all this stuff. I'm usually a bit more reserved."

"It must be the safety of the darkness and the understanding of a fellow traveller." He wrapped his arm around her and she rested her head on his shoulder. They sat quietly for a long time.

Someone set off some bottle rockets. They turned to watch.

"Ready to go back?"

"Yes. Hey, thanks for listening and being a shoulder."

He hugged her shoulders then stood up, offering his hand to help her up. They headed back to the light of the beach fires. Matt kept his arm around her. As they neared the light, he pulled her close, kissed her cheek and said, "Step into the love and light, Jules. You'll never regret the change it makes in your life."

He led her to the circle Cass, Ryan and Ethan had settled in with friends. She sat in an empty chair beside Cass and Matt sat a few people away. Cass looked at her. She looked back and smiled. Satisfied she was okay, Cass turned back to the conversation with Kit on her other side.

Jules was unaware Ethan had watched her and missed nothing when they returned together. He glanced at Matt as he sat down, then looked at Jules for a long time. He tucked away his thoughts for another time.

Around 11:30 Jules caught a glance between Ryan and Cass, and they stood up together. Ryan said, "Well everyone, I think it's time Cass and I headed home." *Oh to be with someone who understood you with just a glance.*

Cass followed with, "Thanks, everyone, for a wonderful evening."

Ethan got up and said, "I think I'll head back with you."

Jules decided to join them. While it had been fun, it was also an emotionally draining night and she was ready for bed. The group strolled back as Cass and Ryan chatted about the evening. On the driveway Jules said, "Really nice to meet you, Ryan. And thank you all for including me in a great evening. You are all very blessed. Good night."

They all answered, "Good night."

Once in bed Jules replayed the evening starting with the "Sweet Caroline" dance with Ethan. She smiled. One week here and they all warmly welcomed her into their lives.

Despite her emotional outpouring to Matt, she had a good evening. She pondered what came over her to spill out her thoughts to a stranger. The contrast of the dark night and deep waters of the ocean with the warm fires and welcoming people caused her to see the darkness in her life, and that she was nearly drowning in abysmal loneliness. And yet steps away were life and light.

Saturday, June 17

I'm drowning. No, not drowning. How did I describe it to Matt? Oh, yes. I'm starving. Starving for the love and deep satisfaction offered by a loving family. Starving not for a mate or partner in life, but starving for the rich companion-ship of family.

I see now my heartache is deep desperation for family. The more I watch Ethan, Cass, Ryan and Matt, and the towns-people, I realize I have longed for a loving family for a long time. Fundamentally, it's not a marriage or boyfriend I've been looking for. I believe I'm starving for a brother, a sister, parents that care. Every year I hear the complaints of colleagues suffering through yet another family meal. They are so glutted on family, they have no idea what it's like to be without. They complain about being too full of family, and I'm starving.

The beauty of Edisto is the people are like family to each other. They appreciate their time together. Oh, to be a part of such a people. I don't know if I'll belong here, especially after four short weeks, and if I do, then how will I rip myself away to try and find it again elsewhere?

I can picture my soul as emaciated and near death, and that's a very accurate picture of my state.

I wonder what it would take to step into the light as Matt suggested. He said I would never regret it.

What was it Matt called himself? A fellow traveller. He felt like a big brother. He was very sweet and caring. Most men would run at the first sign of an emotional woman. But he fearlessly jumped in and really helped. Just knowing I'm not the first to feel this way is comforting. Anders would have me thinking this was just me being weak and too sensitive. Not Matt. It felt good to have his understanding and encouragement.

My word for today is Starvation.

Chapter 8 | Redemption

Sunday, June 18

She awoke late Sunday morning and lay in bed thinking for a long time. She needed to face and deal with her starving soul and spirit. She just wasn't sure how. *Perhaps if I get a chance, I'll ask Matt.*

She made a cup of tea and headed to the veranda. All was quiet. Ryan and Ethan's vehicles were gone. She concluded they had gone to church and thought Matt probably went with them.

There were a pile of books stacked beside her door with a note on top. She took the books inside and opened the note.

"Hope you enjoy these as much as I did. Let me know if you run out. I've got quite a few more. Ethan."

This place is overflowing with men with big and open hearts. For a moment she wondered if she'd landed on another planet. Reading the back covers, she sorted them in the order she wanted to read. She laughed at herself for being so orderly.

She got ready for the beach and grabbed the top book, looking forward to a quiet day with sand, surf and suspense.

After swimming and bodysurfing for about an hour, she read a few chapters of the first book. She heard a dog bark and looked up.

A man threw a ball into the water and a Labrador retriever bounded into the waves to retrieve it. She laughed at its antics, the unbridled joy the dog found in chasing a ball, and she found the way the man enjoyed this moment with his dog endearing.

She watched as the two made their way down the beach. She'd only been there a week and in that short time she'd fallen in love with the place. Looking out to the ocean, she thought about the evening before. The water had been a black abyss, a reflection of the loneliness in her soul. The stones of the secret dune were partly right. Not only did the ocean reflect the mood of the day, but last night it reflected the state of her soul.

She thought about her grammy, trying to recall anything that loving woman tried to teach her about Christianity. She remembered going to church, but not much of what was taught there. She knew her grammy prayed for her. She told her so many times. At her grammy's invitation she'd confessed she was a sinner and accepted Jesus as her saviour, but that was late in her last summer with her. She never had time to learn what that truly meant or to learn of Christian living from the one person in her young life that actually bubbled with Christian life and love.

She set down the book and closed her eyes to think. In a few minutes she was asleep.

She awoke to the sound of kids playing in the water nearby. She noticed someone had placed their towel beside hers and looked around. She didn't see anyone she knew. They must have been very quiet for her not to have heard. She carefully looked at the people in the water. She didn't see anyone who was alone. Further out were a few surfers. She watched them for a minute. They were all resting on their boards, waiting for the next wave. One leaned forward and began paddling. He caught the wave as it rose up. With momentum he stood up. He was pretty good, navigating the wave to its fading, bubbling foam. As he neared she could make out his features and finally recognized him. It was Matt.

He hopped off the board, picked it up and started to come her way.

"Hey, you're pretty good!"

"Hey, sleepyhead. I've lived on one coast or another most of my life and love the water. So I've surfed for almost as long as I've walked. How are you feeling today?"

"Good. I've been thinking about what you said last night about stepping into the light. What did you mean?"

He set the board down and sat next to her. He looked her in the eyes. "I'm talking about committing your life to Christ. I'm not talking about superficial and meaningless Christianity, but living deep rooted in the Bible and walking on the paths of God. I imagine Auntie Peggy told you about Jesus?"

"Yes, but it was so long ago and I was so young, I don't really remember much. I know she prayed for me, and during our last summer together I prayed with her that Jesus would save me, but I don't really know what that means or what it means for me today."

Matt told her of his story, explaining sin and redemption. He told her of the love of God to offer a way to be saved from eternal death and to live in perfect love, peace and joy.

Jules' eyes filled with tears. "I've not lived in a good way. I just left a common-law relationship."

"It doesn't matter how good or bad you've been. We are all sinners and need Him to save us from the cost of our sin." He looked at Jules. "He loves you, Jules. More than you can know. And He's holding out His hand to you, personally offering you a relationship with Him. That's what I meant by stepping into the light. And like I said, you won't regret it."

Tears dripped down her cheeks. Looking down she nodded her agreement.

"Would you like me to pray with you?"

Looking at Matt with brimming eyes, she nodded again. He scooted closer, put his arm around her and bent his head beside hers. He thanked the Lord for her life and His call to her to accept His gift of eternal life. Together they confessed their sins, asked forgiveness and she accepted Christ as her Lord and saviour.

When they finished praying she briefly rested her arm on his knee. "Thank you, Matt." He hugged her close and kissed her cheek.

"God brought you back here for a divine appointment with Him. You are now and forever a part of the best family on earth. You'll never be alone again. Now you have the joyful and challenging walk of a Christian before you. Read your Bible and dig into all that God says. It's His love letter to you and is well worth reading and rereading like you would a love letter from a beloved. Do you have a Bible?"

She lifted her arm from his knee. "No, but I'll go into Charleston this week and get one." Thinking for a moment she said, "You're a software developer, right?"

He took his arm from her shoulders. "Yes, I have both a computer engineering and business degree. And I got into the mobile app business early on. I've developed quite a few, selling many directly to users, and I've sold the rights to three to large corporations. So God has blessed my talent."

"Where do you live when not on a break?"

"I'm down in Houston. Been focused on apps for the oil and gas industry, but I've been thinking of a change. I have a few ideas. Just not sure what the right one is yet. I hope to have it figured out by the end of the summer."

"Hmm. This seems the summer for people to come to Edisto to get their life direction sorted. You, Ethan and I are all in the same boat."

Laughing, he said, "I hadn't thought about it, but yes, it looks like we are all seeking the right path forward. How about you? Where do you live?"

"I shared a small apartment with a guy named Anders in New York City. But most of the projects I work on are up and down the Eastern Seaboard. I suppose I really could live anywhere. I don't think I want to stay on in New York now. I guess that's one more thing I'll need to sort out this summer."

He bumped his shoulder into hers. "If you can live anywhere, why not Edisto?"

"Ha! We'll see."

He laughed out loud. "You sounded just like Auntie Peggy. She always said, 'We'll see,' when she actually meant, 'I don't agree, but it's not worth a disagreement.'"

Smiling brightly she said, "I like to think I've got some of Grammy in me."

"From what I can tell, you have a lot of Auntie Peggy in you."

"What do you mean?"

He paused a long moment, pondering what and how much to say about what he knew of her family roots. "Auntie Peggy was a special woman. She overcame a lot in her past. She was a strong, yet warm, loving and generous woman."

"You see me as strong?"

"I think you have strength you've not tapped into. If you don't think you've got strength, you've bought into a bunch of lies about yourself. And you now have the strength through Jesus to overcome all of this wrong thinking and find that person tucked away inside."

She sat quiet for a long time. He waited patiently, knowing the value of processing silence.

"How is it that you're not married yet? You must have women falling at your feet."

"Wow, aren't you good for a man's ego! No, I don't have women falling at my feet. About a year ago I met a very special gal. Her name is Jessica. She's a nurse at the hospital and volunteers with Samaritan's Purse. She's a stunner inside and out. We've been seeing each other whenever she's available. She's off to Africa for the next couple of months. I miss her, but we Skype at least three or four times a week."

"She sounds wonderful."

"I hope when she comes back from Africa she can spend a week or two here and meet the folks here. I haven't said anything to anyone yet because we don't know if she can change the flights with Samaritan's Purse."

"Okay, I won't say anything, but I hope I can meet her."

"Me too." Watching the waves he said, "Have you ever surfed?"

"Does bodysurfing count?"

"Sort of."

"Then yes, I've sort of surfed."

Laughing, he said, "Want to learn? We have all summer. And I have access to a whole collection of boards."

"Okay, if you think you have the patience."

"Lady, I've got all summer and could use a project. The waves are a bit big today for learning. I'll check the wind report for the next few days. There's bound to be a good day to learn."

"What are you looking for with the wind? What makes the conditions just right?"

"If the wind is coming in from the ocean – onshore – it pushes the waves down and they fail to rise up high enough for surfing. When the wind is offshore it blows into the waves and holds them up, making for a good ride in. To some extent the harder the wind blows, the higher the wave. Here in South Carolina when the wind makes the dunes moan, it makes for a good day for surfers. We'll be looking for a day with a lighter wind coming over the dunes."

"Oh. Listen, if the waves are good for you today, don't feel you need to hang around the beach with me. I've got a good book. Go enjoy yourself."

Patting her knee he said, "You're a keeper. You must have men falling at your feet."

Laughing, she said, "No need to charm me, cowboy. Go play in your waves."

He jumped up, grabbed his board, winked at her and said, "I'm no cowboy, but you can call me a brilliant Bajan, if you like."

"Yeah, okay, sugar cane." Laughing, he left.

She watched him for awhile. *He's a good man. Jessica is a very lucky woman. I hope she doesn't break his heart.*

Chapter 9 | Reminiscing

She picked up her book and opened it to the page marked with her folded piece of paper. She opened the paper to read what she'd written.

My Tribute
The One who paints in colour and clouds,
The One who draws out the paths for the wind to follow,
The One who created the ocean as a mirror reflecting the mood
of the day,
The One who motivates the sea to dance and sing."

When she wrote the words, she'd focused on their beauty and the nature aspect. As she read them again, the fullness of meaning finally dawned on her. She finally saw the obvious. The writer was not only appreciating the wonders of nature, but turned their eyes to the One who created it all. She thought the words all the more beautiful. *This must be a Christian writer.* Again she pondered who it could be. She thought she should go check again to see if there was a new stone.

She made her way into the dunes, heading for the one she called the secret dune. She hurried when she saw a sixth stone. She leaned forward to read, "The One who shapes the dunes to drone a lonesome tune."

Oh, I like this one too. These dunes do weep! I'm not the only one to hear their lonely cry. Matt mentioned the dunes moaning and now this writer called it a lonesome tune. Lonesome – that's a perfect word. She felt a wave of pain from the night before – her starving soul born of lonesomeness.

Her thoughts drifted back in time to her 14th summer. Her cold, disinterested father brought her back here to sell her grammy's home. It was his own mother, but he seemed to not shed a tear for her passing. Jules grieved deeply, but couldn't express it to her father. It all seemed an inconvenience to him.

As soon as they arrived in town, her father stopped at the real estate agency and instructed them to sell the place, including the furniture. He then arranged for some folks to come and clean out all of her personal belongings. Jules sat quietly, listening to the arrangements. She decided to collect her grammy's most prized possessions hidden in the back of the third drawer of her dresser. She'd come across the stash of sentimental things the previous year by accident.

They'd be staying in the house for a week to clear the place out. The first moment she could slip away from her father's eyes, she took the jewellery box, an envelope of snapshots, a lone key and an old shoe box from the back of the drawer. She hid the collection in her luggage and never told anyone of her treasures.

On their last day she awoke to a dark grey stormy sky. It matched what she felt inside. She went to the beach to pour her heart out to the vast looming sky. As the storm approached the wind stiffened and she tucked in-between the dunes for shelter. She slowly wandered away from her grammy's home. She came to a dune with grasses and sea oats blowing in the breeze on top. The wind gusted, blowing through the stiff reeds creating a low moan. She sat down thinking the dune sympathized. As she cried out her heart, the land grieved with her. When her young heart had cried out the pain of her loss, the clouds broke open and poured out their tears.

To this day, she had never experienced such sympathetic charity and compassion from anyone or anything for her circumstances. Certainly not her father, nor any man she'd had a relationship with. Then warmth filled her heart. Matt said she'd never be alone again. The Creator of those storm clouds, the dunes and grasses, and the wind brought together a moment when nature sympathized with her. That same Creator now lived in her life. She realized Jesus had been with her, even back there on that last day at her grammy's home. Looking back, she really felt Jesus had expressed His sympathy through the dunes and poured out rain to weep His understanding for her.

Turning back to the stones, she wondered again about the writer. *Did they have a time in their life when Jesus rounded up nature to mourn with them? What event prompted such deeply moving thoughts? What caused them to hear the lonesome song of the dunes? Who is this person who hears the songs of the land and sees their Creator in nature?*

Standing up she thought, *Could it be Matt? He spoke of the dunes moaning. No, that's impossible. There were several stones here before he arrived. Funny that both the writer and Matt mentioned it. This isn't just a secret dune. It's a weeping dune.*

The memory of all of nature weeping with her young heart, and this poem that seemed to be coming from the depths of another soul brought about a determination to figure out who the author was. She wanted to get to know this person and their story.

She went back to her towel, deep in thought. Although she sat absently watching the surfers, thoughts of the last days in her grammy's house, the storm and the weeping dunes held her attention. After a few hours Matt returned tired and happy. They sat and talked a long time about his youth and his time in Barbados and Edisto.

Chapter 10 | Adoption

Shortly before 5 p.m. Matt said he needed to get back for a Skype call with Jessica and asked if Jules would like to meet her. She said she didn't want to intrude, but he said it was going to be a quick call. It was 1 a.m. there and she was just getting off work. She smiled. *Kind of neat that he wants me to meet his girlfriend.*

Matt and Jessica chatted for a few minutes about her day, then he introduced her to Jules, letting her sit in his chair and he moved to the couch.

Jules said, "I've heard all about you. It's good to meet you."

"You too. I hope to finish my leave with two weeks in Edisto, so maybe we'll get the chance to meet face to face. If not, you'll have to come to Texas and stay for a visit."

"You're working for Samaritan's Purse in Africa? What are you doing?"

"The team's here in South Sudan providing medical support in a refugee camp. Oh Jules, it could break your heart to see all the suffering here. I pray every day for the Lord's protection on my heart and mind. If not for Him I'd be a puddle of tears and useless for His service. Every day there are new arrivals running from the conflict with Sudan.

"There's an amazing Egyptian doctor here, Dr. Atar. Doc's been here 16 years and is the happiest Christian I've met. And he cheerfully works long hours, giving his all to these people. He's such an inspiration to me. I've come back here every year for the past three years and just love the work. Then I come home exhausted and need a vacation for a couple of weeks. So I'll be ready to spend some time relaxing on the beach there. Enough about me, what do you do?"

"Oh, nothing so kind and generous as you. I'm on a break from working on software projects. We implement new accounting software for firms and I bring accounting expertise to the project. We're between projects, and I decided to come here for the summer. I spent my summers here when I was young, so it feels like I've come back home. It's just been over a week now, and I've fallen in love with the place and the people here."

They chatted for a long time. Matt listened for a few minutes, thinking it was amazing how women could find so much to talk about. It was clear they would be talking for awhile yet and he went to the kitchen to make his dinner. He came back 15 minutes later to hear the two of them exchanging contact information and making plans to talk again.

He sat down in front of the computer to close off the call. "Love you, babe. Let me know as soon as you can about whether they can get your return flights changed."

Jules headed back to her place to give them some privacy. An hour later Matt knocked on her door and she called him to come in. "Jess says you two hit it off."

"Yes, she's as wonderful as you said. I'm happy for you."

Matt looked at her for a moment. "Put your trust in God, Jules. He will put someone great in your path when the time is right. But hold out for His provision. In the meantime focus on your relationship with Him. He promises to be closer than a brother."

"Speaking of brothers, over the last couple of days you've become like a big brother to me. Thank you for taking time for me. You've given me good advice. You've introduced me to God and Jesus. And you've opened the door to your life and invited me in to meet the people important to you."

"Big brother, huh? I guess you don't have much in the way of family and I never had any brothers or sisters growing up. Consider yourself adopted. But know as your big brother I get final approval of any guy that comes along wanting to date you."

"Maybe you should. I'm lousy at picking."

"Hey, I'm teasing. If you're going to be my little sister, then we'll need to work on you dishing it back. Listen, I've got a bud who has a couple of kayaks we can borrow and paddle into the salt marshes, if you want. If we're quiet, we'll see all kinds of wildlife. Interested?"

"Oh, that sounds great. I haven't paddled a kayak before, but how hard can it be? Looks like this is the summer for you to teach me every conceivable watersport."

"Good! How about tomorrow or the next day?"

"Either afternoon works for me."

"Okay, let's plan on tomorrow. If you are really interested in all the possible watersports, we can borrow a couple of Jet Skis and take them out to play in the waves."

"Surfing, kayaking, Jet Skis! You're going to keep me busy and exhausted this summer!"

"Nah, I'm just looking after my new sis."

"And you've already done that. I feel a peace in my heart I've never known before since we prayed. I didn't expect to feel so – at rest and so assured I've made a good decision. Thank you, Matt."

"You've already thanked me. It really has nothing to do with me. What you feel is the benefit of God's presence. He is the source of pure love, joy and peace. What you feel is His presence."

"You are the one who pointed me in the right direction. I would never have found God on my own. It really is the greatest gift anyone has ever given me, and I want you to know what you mean to me for doing that."

"You're right and you're welcome, my girl."

Ethan kept his extra tools locked in a walk-in storage area on ground level underneath the rental apartments. He needed his painting tools for work the next day. He had a collection of tarps, brushes, rollers and extension poles set out, and was inside looking for his brush cleaner. Once he found it, he locked them in the truck bed and came back under the house to reorganize a bit.

When finished he closed the doors and locked up. He heard Jules' door open above and Matt and Jules come out.

"Okay. When you get back from working tomorrow, just come on over. When did you say you'd be back?"

"Around noon, I think. Thanks, Matt. I know we met only a couple of days ago, but you've become very special to me. I can't believe all that's happened in our short time together. You've changed my life and I'm so grateful."

"Right back at ya, my girl. Remember, I'll always be here for you."

Ethan felt a bit guilty to have overheard their conversation. After he heard them each return to their own apartments, he took a deep breath and held it for a moment, looking down the road to the ocean. His brows knit briefly. Then he let his breath out slowly. He nodded to himself, committing to something in his mind. He finished up and headed unseen to the beach.

In bed she thought about the significant change to her life.

Sunday, June 18

Redemption – with Matt's help and guidance, I stepped into the light. I have left the dark waters behind. Matt prayed with me and I know I have something special. I no longer stand in the glow of another's light, but I have my own light of Jesus glowing inside me. It's hard to put in words. The light is God inside me. He shines His warm light into all my dark, dismal, hidden areas. I feel like I'm a whole and new person. The former me, Juleena, is but a shadow of the new me – Jules.

I really like being called Jules. It's part of the shedding of the old me.

I think my first real experience with God was back when I was a child at the weeping dune. Maybe He's been with me all along, just waiting for me to invite Him to be a part of my life.

I'm trusting Jesus to give me the strength to overcome my fears and failings. Tonight, my heart sings.

Oh, and I thank God for my new brother. Matt and I kidded about adopting each other, but I think we both meant it. At least I did, and I hope he did too. I feel I belong – I belong to God and He has filled me, and I belong to Matt, someone who knows about being adopted.

Oh, the relief from heartache is amazing. I cannot put into words how it feels to be in the light. It's like I've stepped out of a thick puddle of used oil and have been washed clean, and my empty shell has been filled to the brim. I feel exuberant joy and contented quiet at the same time. Thank you, God, for your redemption. Thank you, Grammy, for giving me a place of roots and memories worth reminiscing. Thank you, Matt, for adopting me.

My word for today is three. Redemption, Reminiscing and Adoption.

Chapter 11 | Love Letter

Monday, June 19

The next morning Jules was up bright and early, and drove to Kit's home. She lived on a larger property a couple of miles inland from Edisto Beach. She parked in front of the barn as instructed. The barn doors were open and she entered to find Kit at work assembling an elaborate hanging light. Kit cleaned off her hands and greeted Jules. They chatted for a couple of minutes about the barbeque.

Kit showed her around her workspace and her creations. Jules fell in love with a beautiful glass bead pendant from her beach series. She showed her how she took pieces of coloured glass and glass rods, melted them, then slowly cooled the bead in a kiln to create colourful and near indestructible glass.

She then took Jules to the office at the back. The property backed onto Fishing Creek. She could see through the trees with hanging Spanish moss to the water. It was a beautiful property and she understood why an artist would live there.

They sat down to go through the paperwork and set Jules up with access to Kit's online books. Looking over the work Jules was confident she could complete the banking, pay the bills and prepare the invoices by the end of the morning. But she soon realized she would probably need to come back another day to clean up some errors. Kit had cut several cheques to various shipping companies, but it looked like they were allocated incorrectly.

They took a break midmorning. Kit brought her an iced tea and gave her a tour of her property. She had inherited the farm from her father several years ago. She converted the barn to a working studio with a furnace for glass blowing, a couple of kilns, several work tables, lots of shelves and a large propane tank out back.

Once she finished the bookkeeping, she took Kit through the completed accounting work and showed her the problem with the allocations. Kit confessed she wasn't sure of what she was doing. Grateful for Jules' help, she gladly made arrangements for her to come back the following week to fix the errors and catch up on any new work.

On the way out she purchased the pendant she noticed earlier. It looked like the sand and surf of Edisto. She slipped on the silver chain and looked in a nearby mirror. *I now have a piece of Edisto of my own.* She liked it so well, she decided to wear it for the summer.

She got back home a bit before noon, changed and knocked on Matt's open door. He was ready, grabbed a large pack and locked up. They drove to the marina and he led her to the docks.

"I thought we were kayaking today. You're taking me to all the fishing boats."

"My buddy Mike is going to take us and the kayaks up to the entry of Mud Creek. I thought since you are new to kayaking, you'd appreciate the lift. There he is," and he waved at a slim man about Matt's age.

They boarded a good-sized and well-equipped sport fishing vessel. Mike offered them a cold drink out of the cooler and fired up the engines. It was a short drive out Big Bay Creek and up the inlet to the entrance to Mud Creek. They dropped the sit-on-top kayaks in the water and the two men helped Jules get into hers without taking a spill. Matt handed her the double-bladed paddle and she drifted away from the boat to experiment with using it.

Matt got into the other kayak and pushed away from the boat. "Thanks, Mike!"

"Give me a call if you want a pickup."

"Thanks. We should be back by 5 p.m."

"Okay. Have fun!"

Mike slowly pulled away. Matt watched Jules for a minute, then paddled up beside her. "Try powering the paddle with your shoulders instead of your arms. You won't tire as quickly. And rotate your shoulders a bit more when you switch sides." She gave it a try. "Looks good! Ready to go?"

"Lead on."

Matt was in the lead when he heard a small splash behind him. He turned back, looking for signs of something moving under the water and spotted the unmistakable ripples. "Watch over there."

Jules spotted the small bow wave and followed it. Two dolphins surfaced and blew air out of their blowholes. She and Matt drifted, watching their playful antics. They swam around and under their boats before swimming out to the bay.

Jules enjoyed the day more than she expected. They saw herons, ibis, egrets, all kinds of songbirds, ducks, a family of otters, turtles and in one of the thickets they saw a pair of young foxes. Matt brought bottled water and snacks in his pack and they stopped frequently to drink, snack and enjoy the wildlife. Heading back was easier as they could drift in the current and still make progress.

They paddled into the marina at 4:52 p.m. Jules easily navigated around the boats' wakes and managed to paddle ashore and get out gracefully. Matt carried the kayaks back to Mike's boat one at a time and they both thanked him for their use. Once in the car Matt said, "I don't feel like making dinner tonight. Want to go out?"

Jules could feel her muscles stiffening and knew she'd be sore the next day. "Sounds good to me."

They decided on McConkey's and ordered a couple of burgers and fries. They talked about their afternoon, plans for the week and sailing with the Thomas family on Saturday.

Tuesday, June 20

On Tuesday morning she got up early knowing Cass and Ethan were generally up and working by 7:30. She knocked on the door and saw Ethan coming down the hall with a thermos and lunch bag in one hand, a coffee and keys in the other, and two pieces of toast in his mouth. Mumbling past the toast he said, "Hey Jules. Come on in. Cass is in the kitchen."

"Thanks for the stack of books. I'm already into them. You're right, Brad Thor's a good writer."

"You're welcome."

She held the door for him and he thanked her on his way out.

Cass greeted her while making a second cup of tea. "Here you go," she said, handing her the second mug. "Oh, before I forget, we have movie night every Wednesday and I want to offer a standing invitation to join us. This week is the anything goes night where we pick something that doesn't fit into chick flick, mystery/suspense or action/adventure."

"Thanks! I think I can fit that into my busy calendar."

Pressing her hand to her heart, Cass said, "I'm glad we booked you before your schedule filled up!" and they both laughed. "Now to business. Here are all the papers and receipts. And I've recorded all the transactions we've done this month on these pieces of paper. Oh, and here's a list of all the companies we have maintenance agreements with that need an invoice."

Laughing at the stack of paper, Jules said, "I'm not sure you need me, Cass. It looks like it's well in hand."

They looked at the pile and both laughed. "Trust me, we need you."

Cass got her logged in and she took a few minutes to look over their accounts. "I don't think this will take long." She had a few questions, but was finished all the work by 10:30 a.m.

"Don't forget to send me your bill."

Jules laughed. "Don't worry, I know where to find you."

She decided to drive into Charleston and pick up a Bible. It would take less than three hours. As she drove she thought over the options of how to invoice and receive pay for the accounting work. She thought it funny that it hadn't occurred to her yet, but she hadn't thought about invoicing. She decided she needed her computer to generate invoices so she could get paid. But how would she get the laptop here? She was reluctant to let Anders know where she was, but she'd need him to at least get the computer out of the apartment.

Then in a flash of wisdom she decided to ask her colleague Susan if she would mind dropping by to pick it up from Anders and ship it from the office. She just lived a block away from their apartment. And she was sure her friend wouldn't mind helping her out. She'd looked after Susan's cat every time she went on holidays.

Once in Charleston, she called the office from her cell and spoke to her friend to confirm she was willing before making arrangements with Anders. The only time she could stop by was that evening. They chatted for several minutes while Jules gave her an abridged version of what was going on.

After she ended the call she closed her eyes and prayed. "Okay, God. I'm asking for your help. Matt says you stick closer than a brother. I could sure use that kind of help now. Please give me the right words to say. Thank you." She took a deep breath and called Anders on his cell.

"Juleena! Where have you been? I've called about a hundred times! What do you think you're doing, walking out on our vacation? I thought we were going to work things out! Next thing I know you've turned tail and run – in the middle of the night like a scared little child! What's the matter with you? Where are you? I don't understand you at all! Do you know how stupid you made me look? I had to cancel our plans and return home! What's wrong with you?"

She listened to his tirade. He hadn't paused long enough for her to answer any of his questions. She hadn't even had a chance to say hello. Finally when he drew a breath, she said, "Nothing's wrong with me. I just don't want to be someone's punching bag."

"Don't be stupid. You know I was drunk. I didn't mean it. Time to get over yourself and come home."

"That's no longer my home, and I won't be coming back."

"Where are you? We can't talk about this on the phone."

"I've rented a vacation place and I'm going to spend the summer here."

"That doesn't answer my question. Where are you?"

"Anders, I don't want to talk. My mind's made up. Really, you need to find someone who is better suited for you."

"Stop being a little fool – I love you. I miss you. Come on home."

"Anders, you're not happy with me. Believe me. This is for the best."

"Jules, listen. I still want to talk. I promise I'll be good. Can't we just talk?"

"Anders, Susan from work is going to come by tonight to pick up my laptop and iPad. Would you please give them to her for me?"

"If I do, will you tell me where you are?"

"No. I'm not ready to talk."

"Okay. Then when do you think you'll be ready?"

"Don't mock me. You are making fun of how I feel. That's no way to treat me."

"What's happened? You seem different."

"I've decided to pursue my grammy's faith. I've given my heart to Jesus. And through Him I'm finding myself."

"Christianity! Have you found someone else? Who are you with?"

"No, there's no one else. I'm not with anyone, but I have made some new friends. Please Anders. Will you give Susan my laptop and iPad?"

"Sure. But this conversation is not over."

"Thank you for helping me. I've got to go now."

"When will I hear from you again?"

"Bye Anders."

"Call me, Juleena."

"Bye Anders," and she hung up.

Considering how difficult he could be, she thought that went pretty well. "Thank you, Jesus. Please be with him. And please don't let him give Susan a tough time." She and Susan agreed Jules would not tell her where she was until Susan had her things. If Anders harassed her, she could honestly tell him she didn't know where Jules was.

She called Susan back to confirm she could drop by that evening and asked if she would text her when she had her things. She'd leave her phone on for the evening.

She went into the Christian bookstore and asked for help picking out a good starter Bible. The owner was a sweet, matronly woman. "Are you looking for an easy-to-read translation? Or one that gives a more fuller meaning?"

"I don't know. Can you show me both and I'll read a bit, then decide?"

She looked over several options and chose a softcover New Living Translation. The lady included a bookmark for her. It read, "Be true to yourself, help others, make each day your masterpiece, make friendship a fine art, drink deeply from good books – especially the Bible, build a shelter against a rainy day, give thanks for your blessings and pray for guidance every day – John Wooden."

It felt good to have her own Bible. She'd seen her grammy read her Bible every evening before she went to bed. She remembered how worn the corners were and how she'd made notes in the margins. Maybe one day her Bible would look so loved and used. *What did Matt call it? God's love letter to her.* She thanked the woman for her help and headed back home to spend the rest of the day on the beach.

As soon as she set up her towel and lounger for reading, she headed for the dunes. She still had this puzzle to solve. Two days had passed since she'd last checked. Sure enough, there was a new stone. "The One who sketches on the beach in dark and light sand with every tide." She touched the pendant she'd bought from Kit and thought, *she makes beautiful things, but once they're made, she doesn't remake them again and again. But God paints the sunset and dawn, day after day. And He uses the sand to sketch on the beach with every tide, creating something new each time. Amazing. And He paints the sky continuously with the revolution of the earth. All the peoples, all the countries, get their own painting emblazoned across the sky. Now that's a great God!*

Her heart felt happy to think the God of continuous artistry cares about her. He loves her and is now a part of her life. She went back to her beach lounger and looked out over the ocean. Like the poem's author, she loved the sight, sound and smell of this place.

She thought about the conversation with Anders. She'd handled it really well. Normally his words reduced her to tears and he'd dish out more insults. But today his words just rolled off her. They didn't reach her heart. She shuddered as she remembered the emotional torment she'd lived with for so long.

She closed her eyes and took a deep breath. *But now I have you, the One who is closer than a brother.*

After soaking in the feelings of peace and rest, she realized how much change had occurred in her already. Who Anders described on the phone – the child who tucked tail and ran – was no longer her. Looking out to the ocean, she remembered seeing her black emotional abyss and the light and life the others walked in, and realized she too walked in the light and life. The black abyss no longer held her hostage to its whims of torment.

Just like in the days of her youth, she was again Jules the strong and confident, not Juleena the whimpering and brokenhearted. She drew in a deep breath of the salt air. She was her grammy's loved girl, not her father's neglected daughter. And Anders and the darkness, a large portion of Juleena's life, would have no part in Jules' life. Never again would she be Juleena the victim. No, she was Jules the child of God. At least that's what she'd read in the bookstore.

For that afternoon she felt the shedding of the old and dead, and the dawning of the new and alive.

She smiled and opened her book to read.

Chapter 12 | Provision

After dinner Jules turned on her phone and took her Bible to the veranda to read. She hoped for a distraction from the creeping anxiety. She worried Anders wouldn't be co-operative and Susan wouldn't successfully get her things.

Looking at the large and imposing book on her lap, she wasn't sure where to start. She decided it best to start at the beginning. She opened to the first pages and came to the table of contents, then a number of pages about the translation and some scholarly front matter. She kept turning until she got to Genesis 1 and began to read.

Matt came out. "Hey, I see you've got yourself a Bible." He leaned on the railing in front of her.

"Yes. I went into Charleston today. I just wasn't sure where to start."

"I think you might find the Psalms or the New Testament a good place. The Psalms were mostly written by King David, a good man of God, and he expresses his innermost feelings about his challenging situation and his trust in God to protect and deliver him. Then the New Testament is all about Jesus and the way to eternal life."

"Hmm, maybe I should start with Psalms tonight. I called Anders today."

"Oh? How did it go?"

"I asked him to give my work colleague my computer and iPad so she can ship them down here. I prayed about it before I called and he agreed, although reluctantly, I think. I'm worried he won't co-operate and will give Susan a hard time. And then I'll have to go there myself. I'm just not ready for that. I'd rather wait and go there when I've got a place to move to. Then I'll go to get all my things and move out."

Pulling up a chair facing her, his legs stretched out past her side, he said, "Let me see your Bible for a minute." He turned to the middle, reading a bit, then flipping pages. "Here it is. Read verse 7 there."

She looked at the chapter title. "Psalm 138 and verse 7. 'Though I am surrounded by troubles, you will protect me from the anger of my enemies. You reach out your hand, and the power of your right hand saves me.' Oh, that's good." She reread the verse to herself.

"Would you like me to pray with you about the success of this evening?" Jules nodded. He leaned forward and held her hands in his. "Our heavenly Father, thank you for my new little sister and that you drew her to yourself. I will treasure her as your special gift to bring family and fullness into my life.

"We come to you to ask for your help and intervention. You know the situation with Anders, and we ask that you would soften his heart and dissolve any resistance. Give Susan courage and the right words to say. Also, strengthen Jules as she learns to walk in your light, life and love. Tonight, fill her with your peace and assurance that she rests in your provision and protection.

"Thank you for your loving and attentive care in our lives. Because of Jesus and His death and resurrection, we pray in His name. Amen." He released her hands and lounged back in his chair

She sighed deeply, letting out her tension. "Thanks, Matt. I think I like having a big brother and I know I chose a good man for the job."

"You're special to me too. And God will take care of things you cannot."

They chatted about the weather report. He thought there would be a good day for surfing toward the end of the week.

The door opened next door and Ethan came out. Looking over at the veranda, he waved to the two of them and made his way over. "Hey Jules. How are you? Cass tells me you are going to learn to surf this summer."

"We were just talking about starting this week. Matt calls me his summer project. I don't know if I'll be any good."

"I'm sure you're in good hands with Matt. I know him to be a good man." Looking at Matt he said, "You up for another golf game? I was thinking of putting in a few extra hours of work tonight and take tomorrow afternoon off."

"Sure. Do you want me to book us a time?"

"Already done. I took a chance you'd be available. We're booked for 1:30. Meet you here at 1:15?"

"Okay."

"Okay. See you two later," and he left.

Her phone pinged notification of a text message. Seeing it was from Susan, she read the message aloud. "'Red Riding Hood to Bambi. Code green. Mission completed. Please send destination information for package.' Oh, she's hilarious. I'm glad Anders was co-operative. Thank you, Jesus." She was about to send her address then thought she'd better find a place where she could be sure someone would be there to receive it. She told Susan she would send her an address that could receive the package in the next couple of days.

Jules settled back in her chair, more relaxed. Their conversation moved on to talking about their various project successes and challenges, finding they shared a similar career experience. Ethan returned around 11 p.m. and waved goodnight to them. They continued chatting until after midnight.

Tuesday, June 20

The black abyss is gone. The torment is finished. The tormentor has lost his power. God inside me is greater than anything Anders can dish out. God protects me from all the Anders in the world. He is my knight in shining armour. And I am Jules! I am something new, something strong, someone very happy. I can't believe how different I feel. I've got God, Anders. What have you got?

No, I will never go back to that life of darkness. It is time to forget Anders. It's time to look forward to what's ahead and not backward in my past. Matt said God threw all my sin into the sea of forgetfulness. I will try to do that too.

I thought earlier that my present has intersected with my past. That I stood in the intersection of life's junction of people, place and memories, trying to find myself. I thought there were only two paths forward, alone with Anders or alone with myself. Now I've found a third path. One with God. Well, I've made a decision on the road forward. I've seen my green light and chosen God. My first steps on my new road and I'm happy.

My word for today is Provision – God's Provision.

Chapter 13 | Daylight

Wednesday, June 21

In the morning she went to Vicky's home on the inlet side of Palmetto Boulevard, just past Townsend Street. Vicky and her husband lived in an impressive southern mansion on stilts. Vicky was prepared for Jules with all the work organized. Since all Mac's clients used the same software and he set things up very similarly for each client, she quickly got to work.

They took a break midmorning and Vicky took her to the decks out back looking out over the inlet. She mentioned Mac was coming home this weekend and she was hosting a welcome home get-together for him on Sunday night. She said he specifically requested she invite Jules.

"He doesn't even know me. I hope he's not worried about me taking over his clients."

"No, I don't think its anything like that. I think he wants to thank you. Maybe he wants to know how long you can help him out."

"Yeah, we'll see."

Jules looked out to the ocean and noted the calm of the water. When she got back home, she took her inflatable lounger to the beach for the afternoon. To satisfy her curiosity she checked on the poem stones and found nothing new. Even out from the inlet and on the open ocean, the water was relatively calm, and she paddled on the float out past the break to read in the sway of the water.

Engrossed in her book several hours passed before she looked up and found she'd drifted north to Edisto Beach State Park. She paddled in to shore and had to walk almost 2 miles back to her towel. She wondered if there was a way to anchor a float to prevent it drifting. She loved the gentle rock of the waves, but wasn't too fond of a long walk home afterward.

On the way to the golf course, Matt found Ethan unusually quiet. "What's up, bud?"

"What do you mean?"

"You're not saying much. Anything wrong?"

"No."

"How are the renovations going?"

"Fine."

"Okay, now I know something's up with you. What are you ticked about?"

"No, no. I'm not ticked. Just working through some stuff in my head." He thought about the beach party night when Matt and Jules came out of the darkness with his arm around her. And the overheard conversation when Jules told Matt he was special.

Matt interrupted his thoughts. "Is this about me?"

"No, not really. I just need some time to accept the turns life deals us all. I'm fine. Really."

"Well, I have news. My girl Jessica will be coming here for the last couple of weeks of August. I want her to meet all of you guys. She's in Africa on a medical mission for six weeks and she'll be needing a rest by then."

"Who's Jessica?"

"The most gorgeous woman I've ever known."

"You've never mentioned her before."

"I have. I told you guys I recently met a girl."

"I thought you meant – never mind."

"What did you think I meant?"

"Nothing. Forget it."

"Come on, man. We've never been anything but honest with each other."

Ethan looked hard at Matt, then looked ahead. "Jules."

"Jules? No, no. She is fantastic, but my heart is elsewhere. Is that what this is about? Do you like Jules? Man, I'm so sorry to have caused you any grief. We're just good friends."

"I don't want to step in if you're interested in her and she's interested in you."

"It's not like that at all. I came upon her alone in the dark at the beach party. She'd been crying, I think. Anyway, we talked about her life and how crappy it's been. Then she comes here and sees all of you, and was longing for what she saw in your lives. I told her about what it was like when I first came here as the adopted son and saw the same thing. I told her how I discovered what it is you all have. And then I encouraged her to become a Christian. The next day we prayed together and she accepted Christ.

"With a shared experience of sorts, she thinks of me as her big brother and I love her like the little sister I never had. In a silly moment we agreed to adopt each other. Really man, there's nothing more between us. I care about her. I care about what happens to her, and I'll certainly look out for her, but I love Jess. Jules is a good woman, Ethan. My advice is to take it slow. She's had some rough times."

"Yeah, the last thing either of us needs is another failed relationship." Squinting his eyes, looking at Matt suspiciously he said, "So how far does this big brother thing go?"

Matt looked at him and laughed. "Far enough that she's agreed I have final say on any guy that's interested in her. She said she sucks at picking men."

"Hmph."

"Don't worry. You've got an automatic approval."

"Yeah, well the two of you don't need to go talking this over. I can sort this out my own way."

Holding up both hands Matt said, "I won't speak of any of this with anyone again."

Satisfied they had resolved what had been hanging between them, they talked about the work Ethan was doing to renovate his newly purchased home.

Jules was a few minutes late to Cass' for dinner and a movie with the ladies. "Cass, I'm sorry to be late. I took an inflatable to relax in the rock of the waves and read. Next thing I knew I had drifted well into the State Park. Next time I'll need to take an anchor with me. It's a long walk back and I'd still be out there paddling back if the drift was south."

They laughed and Cass said, "No worries. We're kind of informal about when to get here."

Ethan came in as they were helping themselves to the food and they invited him to dig in. As everyone filled their plates, Vicky invited them to the Sunday welcome home get-together for Mac. Phones immediately came out as they marked it on their calendars. She noted Ethan and Cass exchange a long glance.

Jules caught Heather alone at the fridge and quietly told her of the sailing trip Saturday with the Thomas family. She asked if her restaurant offered take out. She was looking to bring both dessert and an appetizer – something special. After Heather indicated they did prepare food for takeout, Jules asked if she could recommend something that would be appropriate for the facilities onboard and the family would enjoy, and if the order could be picked up before noon.

Heather thought for a moment, then suggested a cranberry pecan cheese spread with crackers and vegetables, and sushi. The family often came to the restaurant and she made sushi especially for them. And for dessert she recommended a peach divinity icebox pie. Jules asked if the boat would have a big enough fridge. Heather said she'd been aboard several times and it was a well-appointed kitchen. They agreed for her order to be ready for pickup anytime after 11:00 on Saturday morning.

While the ladies were busy chatting, Vicky pulled Ethan and Cass aside. "I saw you two when I mentioned the welcome home party. Is there something going on I don't know about?" They glanced at each other again. "What's worrying you two?"

Cass said, "Does Mac know Jules will be coming?"

"Yes – is there a problem? Mac specifically asked if I'd invite her. Are you worried he's not happy about her helping with our accounting work?"

"No. It's not that at all. I hope he's well enough to handle a get-to-gether."

"Cass, you asked about Jules specifically. What about Jules?"

Ethan said, "Don't worry about it. I'm sure Mac knows what he's doing."

Looking for the matter to be settled, Vicky questioned them again. "Are you sure it will be okay?"

He said, "Yes, it'll be fine."

Vicky returned to the kitchen to pick up her plate and overheard Cass whisper, "Oh Ethan, if he says anything, it could blindside Jules and her reaction might be too much for him to handle. I'm not sure this is a good idea for either of them."

"Shhh. This isn't our secret to hide or to share. Leave it to Mac. This is his business. And I think Jules can handle anything Mac choses to say. She is Aunt Peggy's granddaughter and has a lot of Peggy's strength in her. And maybe it's time to get the secret into the light." He left Cass to her thoughts and joined the ladies in the kitchen. "So, what movie are you watching tonight?"

Heather said, "We haven't decided yet. Any suggestions?"

They chatted on for several minutes trying to decide, and finally settled on a recent release starring Denzel Washington. They invited Ethan to join them, but he declined saying he didn't want to be the only man at the power meeting of the businesswomen of Edisto.

Before they started the movie, Jules asked the ladies for help. She explained about having her computer shipped here but needed an address where someone would be there during the day to receive it. Maddie said she could use her gift shop address and Cass said she was always sending and receiving parcels. She had a locked box the deliveryman used if she wasn't home. Jules thought that would work out well as it wouldn't inconvenience anyone and she could easily get it from Cass.

She sent Susan Cass' address and expected it would be delivered by Friday at the earliest.

Wednesday, June 21

The joy of friends is immeasurable. I love the tightness between the ladies, yet they are so open and welcoming to me. This place is nothing like the cliques of New York. Maybe I just never met the right people there, but these people seem so different, so warm and embracing. I love being here, being home again.

Another day with manageable emptiness and heartache. I feel I am becoming a whole person. Yes, the healing powers of Edisto lie, I think, in finding God. Although the sand, surf and sky, His handiwork, all support His work in me.

I thought I would have trouble filling my time and be wallowing in loneliness. Not so. I'm looking forward to sailing with the Thomases on Saturday. They knew Grammy so well. I hope to learn more about her and hope they're not disappointed in me when they really get to know me.

Sunday I will meet the accounting man Mac. Vicky said he specifically invited me. Although Vicky says I have nothing to worry about, I hope he's an understanding man and not offended.

My word for today is Daylight.

Chapter 14 | Addiction

Friday, June 23

Jules got home midmorning on Friday. She completed the bulk of the work on Maddie's books at the gift shop the day before. It only took another couple of hours on Friday morning to complete.

Matt came down the stairs from the veranda and said the wind looked really good for surfing. He wasn't sure if it might be a little too strong for her at first, but he expected it to die down a bit as the day passed. He pointed under Cass' house. "We're pulling out the collection of boards to figure out which ones to take. Cass and Ethan are coming with us."

"Are you sure you have enough boards for me? I don't need to go today."

"No, no. There's no shortage of boards. Ryan is a die-hard surfer, so they have a wide selection of boards. He and Cassie have surfed for years now and have multiple boards. We're going to look them over to see if there's one long enough for a beginner and for two people. Then we can take you out with one of us. When the wind dies down a bit, you'll be ready to give it a go on your own."

"Okay. I'll be right over after I change."

While they were rummaging through their water toys, Ryan's car pulled into the driveway. Cass hurried to the car to greet him and they came back, arms wrapped around each other.

Matt said, "Hey Ryan, what are you doing home?"

"The project hit a showstopper bug in testing. There's a quick fix, but it would open up a significant security risk. So the developers are going to need a couple of weeks to fix it, and for the company to complete all the regression testing. Other than a couple of days for a few meetings and code reviews, I'm home for a couple of weeks' holiday. It looks like I came back just in time. What's the wind like?"

Ethan said, "I don't know if the waves will be standing up tall enough for you, but it's a pretty good offshore. We're going to teach Jules, if it dies down a bit."

"Any wave is a good wave. Let me put my stuff inside and change then I'll help you sort out the boards. I've got a couple more in the house. Be right back."

Ethan said, "Grab mine in my bedroom too, would you?"

"Got it."

After Ryan went inside Jules said, "Oh man, I hope I'm good enough for this big an audience."

Cass said, "These guys are great. You couldn't be in better hands to learn. When we were kids Ethan taught me to surf by taking me out on his board. Ethan, maybe you could do that for Jules?"

Ethan smiled, tipped an imaginary hat and bowed low before her. "I would be honoured, my lady."

Wrapping his arm around Jules' shoulder, Matt said, "Hey, if you're taking her out, you be careful with my little sister."

Cass said, "Little sister?"

"Yeah, didn't Ethan tell you? We've adopted each other. That way we're not outnumbered by you two."

Cass looked at Matt and Jules. "Okay, Jules Thomas. Here's a neoprene vest for protection against grinding into the sand, or if you'd prefer, here's a Body Glove wakeboarding life vest. Why don't you hang onto both of these while you're here? You might need them."

Trying on the neoprene vest, she said, "It fits perfect. Thanks."

Matt selected a board for himself and Ethan chose a longer board for Jules. Ryan came out with three more boards for Ethan, Cass and himself.

They waxed the five boards, loaded them onto Ethan's truck and they all piled in for a fun afternoon together.

Ryan and Cass took their boards and headed for the water, holding hands. She looked pretty happy to have her best guy home. Ethan interrupted her thoughts. "Are you okay riding tandem with me?"

"Sure. Just tell me what to do."

Matt quietly watched the exchange, took his board off the truck and said, "If you two are good and don't mind, I'm going to head out. Ethan, if you want to catch a few on your own, let me know and I'll swap boards and take over with Jules."

"Okay, well, how about you borrow my board and leave the old board here for now?"

"Okay, thanks. See you two out there."

Looking at Jules Ethan said, "Ready?"

"Yup."

Once in the water, Jules sat on the front and Ethan lay down behind her to paddle out past the break, then sat up. They watched the others as they waited for a good wave and paddled forward to catch it as it broke. Ethan gave her instructions on what they would do to catch a wave together.

Jules listened closely to his instructions and asked a few questions, then said she was ready. She knelt and looked back at the building waves.

"Okay, let's go for this one." They paddled to build up speed and caught the wave just as it crested. Ethan stood up and leaned on the board to cut across the face. He weaved the board downward to gain speed, then turned again to glide across the shortening face. When the wave decayed, he spun the board back over the fading crest of the wave into the trough behind and sat back down.

"Well, what do you think?"

She turned around with a huge grin. "That was awesome! What a rush! I love it!"

"Good! Said like a true South Carolinian."

They paddled out and caught several waves in. Jules was having the time of her life. Ethan encouraged her to try standing. She thought he must be a pretty good surfer to handle all the unexpected movement of a learner, but it gave her an awesome feel for surfing before she would try on her own. Although they fell a few times, they managed several runs with both of them standing.

On their next run they caught the wave, but so did another surfer who accidentally snaked into them. Ethan tried spinning the board away, but it was too late. The wave knocked them both off the board. Ethan fell back and popped up right away. Jules fell into the churning waters underneath the pounding wave. Disoriented in the spin she finally found up from down. She surfaced coughing when the next wave immediately crashed down on her, causing her to again again to tumble under the wave unable to get her footing.

Ethan quickly grabbed her arm and pulled her to the surface. She came up choking and gasping for air. He grabbed her around her waist, and headed for shallower and calmer waters. She coughed and hacked while he carried her. Once in the thigh-deep, foamy waters he set her firmly down on her feet. He let her cough out the worst of it and asked if she was okay.

The other surfer came over to check on her as well. "I'm sorry, miss. I didn't mean to cause you to spill. I'm just learning and not so good yet. Are you okay?"

Steadying herself against Ethan she nodded and sputtered, "Just a bit of water went down the wrong way. I'll be fine, thank you."

"I'm really sorry."

Ethan said, "No worries. I think we're good. Thanks for stopping. Just watch out. Snaking in can get you a punch in the face by some of the guys out here." When the guy left Ethan took her hand. "Come on. Let's go ashore so you can catch your breath. She nodded. Still coughing a bit she was grateful for his steadying hand. Matt came in to see if she was okay.

"Yes. I just had a bit of water go down the wrong way. Give me a few minutes and I'll be ready to go back out. I can see why you all love it."

"Spills happen to the best of us. It looked like you were having fun, though."

"Ethan's really good at keeping the board steady when I stood up. I hope I can manage on my own."

Ethan said, "Do you think you'd like to try on your own? We can head up the beach where the waves are smaller and I'll set you up for them."

"Okay. Maybe by the time we get there, I'll have caught up with the stray drop of water still in my throat."

Matt asked Ethan, "You good? I can step in anytime."

"No, go on back out. I think we'll head up to where the Gibsons used to live. It's likely to be calmer and fewer people there."

"Okay. See you guys in awhile. Take care of my girl."

Ethan gave Matt a crooked grin and a nod.

He took the long board and turned to head up the beach. Jules asked why they weren't taking two boards. He nodded toward the ocean. "Come on. I don't need one."

"You sure?"

"Yup. Come on."

On the way they chatted about her memories of Edisto as a child. When they found a spot with smaller waves, Ethan put the board on the beach to let her practise before heading out. He showed her the proper paddle position and how to pop up to a stand.

When she'd practised her pop-ups a few times, they headed out past the break. It was shallow enough for Ethan to stand. She lay on the board in the position Ethan taught her and they waited for a good wave. He told her to ride the first few lying down. As she started paddling he gave the board a good push. She rode a couple in and said she was ready to try standing.

It was quite a bit different standing up alone on the board, as she no longer had Ethan to stabilize it. She fell off several times before her first successful ride in. She was ecstatic. She hurried back out and excitedly told Ethan how awesome it was. He just smiled and told her to get ready for the next wave. Over the next hour she managed to catch a dozen waves and rode over half all the way in. Ethan told her she was a natural.

As they walked back to the truck she talked almost non-stop, often touching his shoulder when really excited. He quietly enjoyed her excitement and her building trust in him. They sat and watched the others for another hour until everyone was tired and they headed home.

Ryan asked her how she liked surfing and she beamed from ear to ear, telling of her successful rides and how great a teacher Ethan was. "I think she's hooked. I think we can call you a bunny now."

"Bunny?"

Cass said, "It's what the lads call surfer girls."

"I'm a bunny, then. I can see why people choose to live on the southern coasts. I love the feel of being so close to the water and gliding through wind and wave. I even caught a fast-moving one. I love the speed. This is fantastic!" They all laughed, completely understanding the thrill.

Friday, June 23

First, filled with the light and love of God. Then the joy of friends. Now the powerful, addictive thrill of surfing. Feeling the power and strength of the wave underneath, and the wind and spray on my face, I love this surfing thing. It's another connection drawing me, pulling me, tying me to Edisto – to my home.

Yes, addiction. That is the perfect word. I can tell I'm becoming addicted to Edisto, to the life on the water, to the power and excitement of the waves, to the people. I think this every night, but all of this will be hard to leave. Especially when I've discovered I can belong. This place holds me, embraces me. I hold her, feel her power, enjoy her warmth, rest in her arms. God created heaven when He made this place. And He made me a child of Edisto. My heart really is here. This is the best summer I have ever lived.

And I love my new friends in this intoxicating place. This is my place and my people. Funny how I didn't know either ten days ago. Thank you, Jesus for giving me both.

My word for today is Addiction.

Chapter 15 | Admiration

Saturday, June 24

Jules awoke the next morning stiff and sore, and took a hot shower to loosen her muscles. Cass came by as she was making a tea. She dropped off Jules' boxed-up laptop and iPad delivered the previous day. She said the lads had gone to the boat early with her dad.

A young honeymooning couple had rented the middle apartment and she expected them around 10 a.m. Once they were settled she would be picking up her mom around 11:00. She invited Jules to go with her, but Jules said she had a couple of errands to run and would meet her at the boat. Cass told her the name of the boat was *Reckless Abandon* and which slip to go to, then left to talk to Matt.

Jules stopped by the restaurant at 11:30 to pick up the food. Heather had it all packaged in a couple of insulated transport bags and said to give them back to her on movie night. Jules thanked her and drove to the marina parking out front and walked around to the docks. Ethan saw her coming and met her halfway. He took the packages asking what was inside. She cryptically said, "Food." He helped her onboard and pointed her down to the galley where Sandra and Cass were organizing things in the kitchen.

Jules took the food out of the insulated boxes and handed them to Sandra to put in the fridge. Sandra commented on how good everything looked, thanked her and said the sushi would be a big hit. She asked how she knew to bring sushi and how she knew to bring so much. Jules laughed and said Heather had made the recommendations and prepared the food. To her it looked like too much for the seven of them, but both Sandra and Cass seemed to think it would all be gone by the time they arrived back at the dock.

With three of them working, things in the kitchen were quickly ready for the meals and they went up to the cockpit to enjoy the sail out to the bay. They were about to cast off when an older man came by. "Greg. I was hoping to get a few minutes with you."

"Hey Alistair, when did you get in?"

"This morning. Got a spot of trouble and would appreciate you taking a look. Hi Sandra, Cassie, Ethan."

"Hi Alistair," they said in unison as they stepped forward to shake his hand.

"You remember my nephew Matt?"

"Thought you looked familiar. Hi Matt"

"Hi Alistair."

"And this is Jules Morgan, Peggy Morgan's granddaughter. Jules, this is Alistair MacKenzie, Old Mac's younger brother."

"Much younger brother. Did you say Jules? Aren't you –"

Sandra coughed and Greg said, "Alistair, how about I come and take a quick look now?" He hopped onto the dock and led Alistair away. "What did you say was the problem?"

Back on the boat there was an awkward silence, leaving Jules to wonder what Alistair was about to say that both Greg and Sandra intentionally interrupted. Finally Sandra said, "Alistair and his wife sail up from the Florida Keys for the summer every year to visit with his brother. I imagine they will be at the party tomorrow night."

Greg, now 20 yards down the dock, called back. "Ethan, would you mind joining us? I think this might require your expertise!"

Ethan hopped out and followed the two older men to Alistair's boat. Cass said, "Ethan used to be a champion sailing racer. He can make a boat do things no one else can."

Surprised, Jules asked, "When did he race?"

"He started with local regattas when he was quite young, then in his mid to late teens he was in races up and down the Eastern Seaboard. After high school he went to Australia for several years and was involved in the big international races, winning most. He really knows wind and water. He was considered one of the best sailors in the world, then he walked away from it all and became a minister."

Jules thought about what Cass said and concluded a deeper story lay behind it all. He had told her he kicked around overseas for a few years, picking up odd jobs before going to university. He didn't mention being an international racing champion.

The conversation rolled on to other topics and soon Greg and Ethan returned. Sandra said, "Did you get Alistair sorted?"

Ethan said, "I'm going to take his boat out this week and see what the problem is."

Greg started up the engine, and Matt and Ethan untied the boat from the dock and pushed off before jumping back onboard. They were off. Greg navigated out of the marina and turned left to follow Big Bay Creek out to the inlet. It was a beautiful sunny day. Even tucked in the river, Jules could feel a good breeze and expected they were in for a good wind out on the open water. As Greg navigated along the short distance of the creek, Matt and Ethan removed the sail covers and prepared to hoist the sails.

Once clear of the creek and into the inlet, Greg shut off the engine and the lads pulled up the sails. The steady southerly wind blew filling the sails, and the boat sped across the water. Greg asked Ethan if he wanted to take the helm, suggesting he give them all a thrill and make the boat sing. Jules wasn't sure what that meant, but presumed he was asking Ethan to work his magic with the wind, the boat and the sails to speed them along their way. She'd never been on a sailing vessel before and had been looking forward to the day. She thought the promise of a good day increased tenfold with a racing champion at the helm. She anticipated he could make the boat fly across the water.

"Sing, hey? I think I can do something with this wind." He replaced his dad at the helm and looked for a moment at the top of the sail, then scanned across the bay.

"Ready to come about!"

When Matt and Ryan had hold of the ropes, Ethan commanded, "Helms alee!" Ethan spun the wheel and the boom swung across the deck. "Tighten the sheets to close haul!" Matt eased off his rope and Ryan tightened his, pulling the sail so the boom was positioned over the deck. The wind filled the sail, the boat leaned over onto its side and they picked up considerable speed.

Looking up at the top of the sails again, Ethan said, "Trim the sails a bit more please, Ryan!"

There was a final snap of the sail as it completely filled with air. The boat flew across the water. It leaned so far over that Jules sat out of the water. Her legs stretched out, her feet pressed against the middle of the cockpit to hold her place in the seat. Looking across to the other side she saw the water rushing by close to the edge of the deck. She thought surfing was fun, but this was a whole new kind of fun. She quickly decided sailing could become her passion. She could see why Ethan would love racing. The speed, the snap of the sails, the spray of the water – all were exhilarating.

Ethan called for another change and the boom swung back to her side of the boat. Now she was sitting just off the water and couldn't help but let her hand skim it. She laughed in delight. Ethan looked over. "Good?"

"Fantastic!"

Smiling, he turned back to watch ahead.

They made a couple more tacks and Ethan asked if Jules would like to learn to sail. She smiled like a kindergartener being put in charge of the Oreo cookies. "Okay, come here and take the helm." She stepped up to the wheel taking a hold and keeping it positioned right where Ethan had it. He stood behind her reaching around her with one arm to hang on. With the other he pointed to a landmark across the bay and said to keep the boat pointing at it.

He then told her about the set of the sail and the tells at the top indicating wind on either side of the sail. He talked her through a couple of tacks, showing her how to ensure the sails were set correctly. And then he acquainted her with some of the common names of things, such as explaining the ropes are called sheets.

He pointed out another sailboat approaching from the right and told her to tack to sail in behind it. With a bit of prompting, she managed the commands and steering, much to her delight.

As they neared the far side of the inlet, he took over and they turned to trace along the shore of the bay, shifting from close hauled to beam reach easing the boom out over the water. They now sailed perpendicular to the wind. The boat levelled out and Ethan gave the helm over to Matt.

Sandra brought up the cheese and vegetable tray, and the sushi appetizers. Greg said, "Sushi! I didn't see you bring sushi."

"I didn't. Jules brought the appetizers and dessert."

Ethan looked at Jules and winked at her. "Today, you are my most favourite person in the world. I love sushi."

"And you're why she brought three trays. Help yourselves, everyone." Watching the little rolls disappear, she was glad to have taken Heather's advice. Sandra was right. There would be nothing left before they even left the inlet.

They sailed around the point and turned south. Everyone took turns crewing and they ran for a long distance south. Ethan took over again. Indeed, he could make the boat sing. "Dad, do you still have the spinnaker onboard? If this wind holds, it'll be perfect conditions to fly home."

"Yes, I just replaced the old one with a couple of new ones – one for reach and one for running. I'd love for you to give them a test run."

"Okay. I think we can give them a good workout. Anyone want another turn at the helm?"

Cass volunteered and decided to head out to sea. She ordered the set of the sails and asked for a couple of corrections, playing around with the position of the main and jib sails. Then she asked Ethan for some help.

"On this boat I've found it best to not have the main sail perpendicular to the boat because it just blankets the jib. Let's haul in the main a bit and let out the foresail a bit more." He stayed behind Cass as she ordered the changes and immediately Jules noticed increased speed.

Greg joined his two children at the helm and the three talked over the wind, the tells and the position of the sails. Cass ordered a change in tack and they turned to head back into shore. They adjusted the sails to make the most of the wind. Both Cass and Greg were learning from Ethan. It was interesting to watch. He was a top-notch sailor, yet he wasn't a backseat driver telling everyone how to sail. He waited to be asked, like a gentleman. And he had a gentle way of teaching. Even his dad respected Ethan's skill and wanted to learn from him. They were quite a remarkable family.

By sailing out to sea and back, they made less progress down the coast, but the family considered developing their skills more important than the distance travelled. For Jules, she loved the feeling of racing across the ocean, water spraying in her face, and didn't care where they went. By late afternoon Greg asked Ryan to take them inshore and find a quiet place to anchor for dinner. Jules loved the way Greg made sure everyone had a turn at the helm and yet balanced that with ensuring Ethan gave them a good ride.

As they set anchor Jules helped Sandra and Cass with the multiple salads while the men barbequed steaks. Everyone filled their plates and they all chose to eat on deck rather than at the dining table below. Jules quietly enjoyed the family chatter. When they talked about the intricacies of sailing, she didn't understand the language, but paid close attention to try to glean some understanding of the principles.

When finished the main course, they relaxed awhile before starting on dessert. Ryan and Cass sat alone at the bow, quietly talking and holding hands. Jules felt a pang of loss. She wondered if she would ever find herself a relationship as good – and with such a quality family. Matt had told her to turn it over to God and at the right time He'd give her what she was looking for. She'd have to trust Him, because her record of choosing a mate had been a pretty poor one.

Jules thought after such a big dinner no one would be interested in another bite, but the lads eagerly tucked into a couple of helpings of dessert.

As they started on their way back home, Greg asked Ethan if he thought the wind was still good for a chute. Cass leaned over and said to Jules, "You're in for a treat. Dad never pulls out the spinnaker unless Ethan's here."

"What's a spinnaker?"

"It's like adding a huge billowing parachute to the front of the boat. It makes a huge difference when running with the wind. Dad likes when we sail with it as it can be seen by all the other vessels and it generates talk back at the marina."

Ethan opened the hatch to the sail locker to pull out the running sail. Meanwhile Matt and Ryan pulled down the small sail out front, disconnecting it from the mast and neatly folding it. The two helped Ethan get the new sail attached and hoisted into position. It fluttered in the air as they hoisted it up, then ballooned and snapped full. It was a beautifully colourful sail of blues, reds and oranges. She now understood how everyone around would notice. She looked around at the other sailing vessels and noted they were the only ones with a spinnaker. And as Cass said, it made a considerable difference to their speed.

Although Greg was at the helm, Ethan spent quite a bit of time beside him as they talked over the nuances of setting the sheets. They steered into a broad reach, requiring adjustments to the sheets and more conversation between the two. Once Greg seemed comfortable managing the helm, Ethan sat beside Jules. "So, how do you like sailing?"

With a big smile she said, "You know how I was excited about surfing?" He smiled and nodded. "Well, this is way more fun. I love the speed. And I love watching the water zip by."

"Good!" He leaned back into the seat, stretched out his legs and rested his arm on the rail behind her but the next moment he sat forward. "Come on. I think you'll like this." He took her hand and helped her to the bow. She carefully navigated past the sheets and stepped onto the cabin top, hanging on tight to Ethan to steady herself. She couldn't see ahead, but when he got past the mast he brought her up beside him. "Look," he said pointing to the bow wave over the edge.

A pod of bottlenose dolphins raced with the boat and jumped over the bow wave. Jules turned to Ethan. "They're beautiful."

"Want to sit down on the edge and watch? They'll probably race with us for awhile." Nodding, they sat with their legs dangling over the edge, leaning on the hand rails watching the dolphins play. They sat for a long time talking and watching the dolphins, then watching other sailboats.

After a couple of hours sailing, the sun sat low in the sky. Ethan and Jules took down the spinnaker and put the jib sail back up for the remainder of their journey. Then joined the others in the cockpit to watch the sun set. They arrived back at the marina around 10:30 in the evening. Jules helped pack up and clean the kitchen and they were home shortly after 11. When she thanked Sandra and Greg for sharing their day with her Sandra said, "We enjoyed having you, my dear. You remind me so much of Peggy. We'll be taking the kids out again soon and we'd love you to come along."

"Thank you. I would love to. And I can see why Grammy loved you all so. You're very generous."

As she lay in bed she thought about her day and how she had enjoyed, for a brief time, family life. An ache welled up in her heart and she rolled over and let the tears spill. "Oh God, it really hurts to see something so wonderful, but know its not mine. I know I have you, but I feel so alone. I don't really belong anywhere. I really need you." She thought about all the years she lived with her father. He never wanted her around, never shared his expertise with her, and certainly there was little love between them. She wondered where he was. Several years ago he moved and never bothered to tell her his new address.

She picked up her journal.

Saturday, June 24

Today was a wonderful day spent with an amazing family. I think this is the first time I've seen how great a family can be. Greg is what I would've liked my dad to be. I can see why Ethan, Cass and even Matt and Ryan all enjoy spending time with him. I wonder what it would've been like to grow up with a father that loved me and I loved back.

It's probably good Anders and I never had any kids. He would not be a good father. No. Now that I think about it, I think he's is a lot like Dad, caring only about himself. Maybe I got into a relationship with him because he's like Dad and that was all I knew. What a difference a good father makes. When I look at Ethan and Matt who both grew up under Greg's leadership, I can see it makes all the difference in the world to the type of man they became. If I ever have kids, I want it to be with a man like Greg who would love and lead them.

Now I understand why Ethan and Cass are such good people.

What kind of woman would turn her back on Ethan and all this family had to offer?

I do ache for all that is missing in my life. But I'm done with the losses of my past. I promised myself to look forward. From today on I will try to not mourn my past but celebrate today, and anticipate tomorrow. The ache still appears, but I won't let it settle in.

And the best thing about today is my discovery that sailing is even more addictive and thrilling than surfing. I didn't think it possible to best the thrill of riding down a wave, but I love the sound of the sails, the speed, the ability to harness nature to fly across that powerful water, to race the waves, to create your own wave that dolphins come play in. Amazing! But it's the sport of people far more wealthy than me. I may need to settle for surfing and take whatever sailing opportunities come my way.

Chapter 16 | Anticipation

Sunday, June 25

Jules awoke late and spent the bulk of the day at the beach. As soon as she found a spot, she went to check on the weeping dune and the poem stones. Excitedly, she spotted a new one. "The One who gives a man love of wind and water, spray of the bow and snap of the sail." She drew in a deep breath. Now she knew it was an adult male writer, and one who sails. She reflexively thought of Ethan, then thought there are many sailors in Edisto. But this narrowed the field of possible writers

Walking back to her towel she thought she would pay more attention to Ethan and to when a new stone appeared.

The day passed quickly and quietly. She left herself time to get home, clean up, and grab a bite to eat before hitching a ride with the lads and Cass to Vicky's for the welcome home gathering for Old Mac. She was putting away her dishes when Matt knocked on her door. "Ready to go?"

She picked up a small wrapped package from the table and Matt held the door open for her. Ryan, Cass and Ethan were already at the car. Cass said, "Did you get something for Mac?"

"Yes. Maddie helped me pick out something."

"Oh that wasn't necessary. I doubt Mac will be expecting anything."

"Maddie said the same thing. The way I see it, Mac knows all of you and just you being there is your gift. He doesn't know me from Adam, so I thought I'd better bring something."

Ryan muttered, "Don't be so sure." Cass elbowed him hard in the ribs.

Jules wasn't quite sure about what he said. "What was that, Ryan?"

Cass said, "Nothing. He's just being a goof."

Ethan opened the back door for her to get in. "Don't worry. I'm sure he'll like whatever it is."

Once in the car she leaned forward. "Cass, is it too much?"

Matt got in beside her and said, "You could give him a jar of saltwater and he'd think it was great."

Ryan burst out laughing and took another jab to the ribs. "Stop it, both of you."

Ethan got in the car on her other side. "Ignore them. We just wish we were as thoughtful."

She looked at Ethan, still concerned. He put his arm on the back of the seat behind her and nodded his silent answer that it would be fine.

Matt said, "Hey Jules. Are you interested in Jet Skiing tomorrow? We can goof around in the inlet, if you like. It'd be less waves." With a bad boy look, he said, "Or we can take them out into the ocean if you're up for the challenge of wave jumping."

"I don't know about the wave jumping part. I've seen videos of guys flying 20 ft. through the air, but the Jet Skiing part sounds like fun. Count me in."

There were a number of cars and golf carts filling the driveway, so they parked along the road. Jules thought half the town must be there too. Then she briefly wondered if the poem stone writer would be there.

Cass and Ryan stopped to talk to friends in the yard as the other three entered the open front doors along with several visitors. Jules could see through to the back, and people were milling about the large entertaining room and on the deck beyond. As they made their way in, Ethan spotted Alistair waving at them. He waved back, but steered Jules in the opposite direction and was grateful to see a couple of people intercept him.

Mac's daughter hovered by the door to greet the guests. She made her way toward them. "There you are! This must be Jules?"

"Hi Celeste. Jules, Matt, this is Celeste Marsden, Mac's daughter. And Celeste, this is Jules, Peggy Morgan's granddaughter, and my cousin Matt Thomas."

"Hi Matt." Matt nodded and shook her hand.

She turned to Jules. "Hi Jules. I would like to personally thank you for your help with keeping Dad's clients' books for them while he recuperates. He would not have been inclined to rest as the doctors ordered if he had to worry about everyone. Dad's looking forward to meeting you. Go on out. He's sitting on the deck."

Jules looked out and saw a number of people around him. "He looks pretty busy. We'll go out when he's not so busy."

"Okay, but he's been looking for you since people began arriving. Please try to fit yourself in as soon as you can. Good to see you, Ethan, Matt. Nice to finally meet you, Jules."

"You too, Celeste."

Ethan asked if she'd like a glass of wine. He left her in Matt's care and waited at the bar. When he noticed Cass behind him, he leaned over to her ear. "Code red!"

"What?"

"Alistair spotted us and looked like he was about to zero in on Jules. I've got her and Matt stashed away in the corner. Go tell him not to say anything to Jules about –" He paused to look around, spotting the town gossip quietly listening. "Well, you know."

"Okay, James Bond."

Straightening up and pulling at his golf shirt collar, he said, "Ooh

115

that's me, alright! Suave, debonair and cool."

"Careful there, young man. You're a minister. Do you really want people thinking you're a ladykiller?"

"Maggie McPherson! How are you?"

The diminutive town gossip moved in close and reached up to his face, giving his cheek a hard tweak. "You are a handsome young man now, aren't you?" Then patting both cheeks she said, "You need to find yourself a good Carolina girl and settle down. Give that mamma of yours some grandbabies."

"Yes, ma'am."

"Hey Ethan. What can I get you?"

Turning to Vicky's husband behind the bar, he said, "Hey George. Two white wines and a red, please."

"You got it. Say, are you here for awhile? I would like to catch up with you and talk about some things going on with my sloop. I've talked to your dad and he said to talk to you."

"Sure, George. If we don't get a chance to talk, just give me a call," and he wrote down his cell number on a napkin.

As he carefully made his way through the crowd balancing the three drinks, he saw Matt and Jules off by themselves engaged in a deep conversation. In his heart he had a flash of anger – not at either of them really. Just that Matt was her go-to person. Then in his heart he heard the Lord check him.

"Don't let jealousy reside in your heart. Jules needs a number of people in her life. I have called Matt to fulfill a role for her and her for him. You need to let him do what I've asked without judging."

"Forgive me, Lord. You are right."

"She will lean on him for a time, but soon she will need someone more than a brother. Be the man I'm asking you to be. And know I have set her on your path. Now go in peace."

"Here are your drinks. How about I introduce you two around? Matt, you probably know most of the people here."

"Yeah, I think I'll go catch up with a couple of old friends. See you two later."

"Ethan, my boy. I heard you were in town."

"Hey Jim. Let me introduce you to Jules Morgan. She's Peggy Morgan's granddaughter."

"Nice to meet you, Jules. Are you in town for vacation?"

"Yes, for the summer."

"She's helping out Old Mac keeping up on the bookkeeping work for his clients."

"Oh, I've heard about that. Good to meet you. I hope Edisto gives you a good summer.

"Listen Ethan, I bought a new cruiser out of Virginia Beach and brought her down last week, but she seems a little sluggish. Would you mind checking her out?"

"Sure, I can probably take her out this week. I might bring along my sailing crew to help out," nodding at Jules.

Winking at Jules Jim said, "Nice crew. That'd be great, thanks. Here's the key. I'm out of town this week, but feel free to take her through her paces."

"What's she called?"

"The *Dark Secret*."

"Okay, I'll leave the key for you at the marina office when I'm done."

"Thanks, my boy." Looking at Jules he said, "Did he tell you he's a world-renowned sailing legend?"

"No, he didn't, but I've heard it from others."

"We're all pretty proud of our boy."

"Thanks, Jim."

"Oh, I see Old Mac. If I don't see you later, thanks again for your help."

Ethan looked at Jules. "Who told you?"

"Cass. Yesterday, when you and your dad went to check out Alistair's boat. You're a bit of a celebrity here."

"Yeah, it seems that way. I haven't been back since my racing days. And I finished racing several years ago now. I thought it would be long forgotten."

"Based on yesterday I'd say you are very good and the reputation is well deserved. I think it's cool that I know an international star."

"I'm no star."

"These people think so. And I watched you yesterday with your family. They all highly respect your talent and opinion. And you're a very good instructor. You're a natural."

"Thanks, Jules. You are good for me. I should have asked, would you mind crewing for me this week? I'll have to check the weather for a good wind day."

Excited, she grabbed his arm. "I'd love to. You'll never have to twist my arm to go sailing."

"Little Jules Morgan! I haven't seen you since you were knee-high to a grasshopper. I heard you were in town. Are you moving here?"

They turned around. Ethan said, "Jules, let me introduce you to Melody Sampson. You might remember her as Melody Brown. The Browns lived next door to Auntie Peggy."

"Melody! I thought of you the other day and wondered if you'd still be in town. I have many fond memories of you. You were so good to look out for me when I was a kid. What are you doing now?"

"Well, I'm married and we have three children of our own, two adopted ones and two foster kids. So I'm living my dream looking after all our babies. So? Vacation? Or are you moving back?"

"Summer vacation. Although I've only been here a couple of weeks and I've fallen in love with the place. It wouldn't take much to tip me over into moving back."

They chatted with a lot of people, many happy to reconnect with Ethan the sailing hero. One older man suggested Ethan forget about renovations and use his God-given talent and teach sailing. Jules couldn't read what Ethan thought of the idea. They both ended up dodging some questions they'd prefer not to answer. After the fifth similar conversation, she concluded that's how it was when you came home to a small town.

Eventually they made their way outside and waited to see Old Mac. When it was their turn, Ethan leaned down to shake Mac's hand.

"Good to see you home, Mac."

"Good to be home again, my boy."

"Mac, let me introduce you to Jules Morgan, Peggy's grand-daughter."

Jules held out her hand and he took it in both of his. "Jules Morgan. I recognized you as soon as I saw you. I've been waiting to meet you. I owe you much thanks for taking care of my business and my friends during my illness. I couldn't have been more pleased when I heard it was you."

"Thank you, Mac. I am happy to help out. You just say the word when you're ready to step back in."

"Sit down where I can see you for a moment. How long are you here for, dear?"

Ethan pulled up a couple of chairs. "I only have plans for the summer. After that, I'm not sure."

He continued to hold her hand while he spoke with Ethan for a moment. His face seemed vaguely familiar. She liked his almost permanent smile lines, the gentleness about his twinkling eyes, and the way his eyes smiled at people as they peeked out from under his bushy brows and heavy eyelids. She understood why everyone loved this man. He was a bit like Santa Claus in his face and his nature.

He turned his attention back to Jules. "I'm pretty tired tonight and I have many people to talk to, but I'd like to invite you over for lunch or dinner one day this week. Can you fit an old man into your schedule?"

"Sure, Mac. Celeste has my contact information. Let me know when you're feeling up to it."

Patting her hand he said, "Good, good. I like you, Jules Morgan. You've grown into a lovely woman. I have something I'd like to show you I think you'll find interesting. Maybe tomorrow or Tuesday?"

"I can come Tuesday for dinner. Would that be okay?"

"How about 6 p.m.?"

"Okay. Oh, I have something for you." She gave him her gift.

"Thank you, Jules. Could you help me open it up?"

She broke open the wrapping paper and handed it back to him. He removed the paper and opened the box. He pulled out a black mug with a big red kiss and the quote, "You don't have to be an accountant to love numbers."

He laughed. "This is perfect. Only two accountants could appreciate a mug like this. Thank you, Jules. Until Tuesday then? And Ethan, you come along as well."

"Okay, Mac. We'll be there. Take care. Bye for now."

"Bye Mac. See you Tuesday."

"Bye, my girl." He released her hand, closed his eyes with a smile and put his head back to rest.

Celeste saw him resting and whispered to Jules. "Thank you so much. You were the one he was waiting for. I think he'll be happy to rest now. Thank you for coming. You made his evening."

Ethan led her through the house and out to the front yard. Jules said, "What do you think Mac wants to show me?"

Ethan saw Matt, Cass and Ryan out by the road. He led her toward the others. "I guess you'll have to go Tuesday to find out."

"You're coming, aren't you?"

"If you'd like."

"I'd like if you would."

"Then I'm coming."

Saturday, June 24

Curiouser and curiouser. Celeste said I was the one Mac was waiting for. Maybe he's just really grateful – but then what could he possibly have to show me? Maybe he knew me when I was a kid.

The more I think about it, the more it seems there's been a cloud of mystery surrounding the entire evening. What had

Matt and Ryan said earlier that got them into trouble with Cass? Oh yeah, when I said Mac knew all of them and their presence was their gift, but I was a complete unknown, so I wanted to bring a gift, Ryan muttered something that sounded like, "Don't be so sure." So sure about what? Mac didn't seem the type to not appreciate everyone coming to see him. And then Matt said I could bring a jar of saltwater and he'd think it was great. What did that mean? I can't make sense of any of it. They make Mac sound dotty.

Anyway, it could be an interesting week ahead. I feel a little stirred up – like there's something big on my path. Anticipation! I don't know whether I should be worried or happy. I think I will choose happy. Had enough of worry.

It's very interesting how many folks want Ethan's opinion on their boats and sailing skills. If Cass hadn't said anything the other day, I'd have no idea he is a well-known international personality. He lives so understatedly. Another score for a job well done by Greg in raising him. I admire Ethan greatly for the way he's handled his talent and fame. Not many people do as well. There's a John Wooden quote that goes something like, "Talent is God given. Be humble. Fame is man given. Be grateful. Conceit is self given. Be careful." I see humility, gratitude and care in Ethan.

I wonder if he'll do anything with his talent. All the guys looking to improve their sailing and understand their boat want his time and advice, even the older guys. I hope he does something with that. He's a good teacher and people always love to learn from someone who knows their stuff, but isn't an egomaniac.

Thank you, Jesus, for bringing me here, becoming part of my life and bringing me into the lives of such good people. I'm learning a lot from them. Please continue to show me what you want me to learn.

My word for today is Admiration.

Chapter 17 | Revelation

Monday June 26

After checking her email and confirming work for Tuesday through Thursday mornings, she made breakfast and took it out to the veranda. Matt was already lounging out there.

"Good morning, Jules."

"Good morning, Matt"

"How are you today?"

"Good."

"Still up for a day of Jet Skiing?"

"You bet! Already got my life jacket waiting at the door."

"Oh, good. We would have had to break into Brad's storage bin to get you one." Finishing his last piece of toast, he said, "So, you finally met Old Mac."

"Yup. He's a sweet man, I think. I like the way his eyes sparkle when he laughs. He invited Ethan and I for dinner. He said he has something to show me."

Looking closely at her he said, "Oh yeah? Did he give you any clue as to what it is?"

"No, nothing. Celeste said I was the one he was waiting for. I don't know what that means either."

When she looked up at him, he broke from studying her face and looked away.

She looked at him a moment. "And what was with you and Ryan yesterday in the car?"

"Nothing. We were just being a couple of goofballs." Giving her arm a light punch, he said, "You've tried wind-powered sports. Today you're going on the sweetest ride of your life. With your love of water and speed, I think you'll find Jet Skiing a blast."

"Okay. You guys haven't let me down yet. As soon as I'm done my yogurt, I'm ready."

They drove out to the country and drove down a long driveway of a home backing on St. Pierre Creek. They found a note on the front door. "Unexpectedly out of town. You'll find the keys to the Jet Skis in the usual place. They're all gassed up and ready to go. Jackets are in the boat. Have fun! And let's catch up over dinner this week. Brad."

They walked down to the dock where six Jet Skis were tied up – a couple of Jet Skis rigged for towing, a couple of cruisers, and a couple of crafts that looked like Ninja racing bikes. Matt retrieved the keys from a hidden box under the tenth board of the dock. He pulled out the keys for the larger Yamaha Cruiser and the Ninja-like Kawasaki.

He gave her some operational and safety instructions, and they were off. The five-minute ride along the winding river gave Jules time to get the feel for the machine. When they arrived at the end of the river, they steered across the inlet for the more calm waters of the far shore.

By midday they headed for Edisto Marina to tank up both the Jet Skis and themselves. Jules spent the afternoon trying increasingly larger waves. Although she took a few spills, Matt admired her courage and determination. She said it wasn't courage or determination. It was sheer joy.

The day passed quickly. When she got in bed, she fell asleep almost immediately.

Tuesday, June 27

The next morning Jules went to Greg's yacht club and marina at 7 a.m. to get an early start on the day. Greg met her in the parking lot and took her to his office. He had laid out the work, now a few weeks' worth, for her.

About midmorning one of the mechanics came into the office looking for Greg. He chatted her up, took her to the dining room for a coffee and eventually asked her out. He seemed nice enough, she felt flattered, but wasn't interested. There was something about him she couldn't pinpoint that led her to decline his invitation. As he walked away she felt a little proud of herself for not jumping at the first offer of a date. She felt strong.

After getting through the majority of Greg's work by noon, she asked when she could come back and finish. He said Mac generally kept up with the bookkeeping biweekly and wondered if that would work for her until Mac was back to work. They agreed she would come back every other Tuesday.

With her work done for the day, she looked forward to some quiet time on the beach to read and think. As usual she went to the weeping dune to check on the poem stones. There was a new one. "I contemplate you and your provision."

She read through all the stones and thought this one was different – like a turning point in the rhythm and direction of the poem. She wondered if this change was always planned or if it was a reflection of a change in the author. That thought made her consider if the writer had already completed this work and was committing his thoughts to stone as a symbol of permanence, or if each stone appeared as he thought of the next line.

The thought of God's provision stayed with her for the afternoon. She considered the lonely life she'd lived in New York. She had Anders and his friends, but she'd still felt alone. *Perhaps that's why I put up with – actually accepted – his torment. I was desperately alone, yet never found a place of companionship in any relationship and I'd given so much of myself in hopes of eliminating the black abyss of isolation.*

But now here, with God in my life, the blackness has been swept away – blown away by the steady South Carolina winds. Yes, it is good to contemplate God's provision. She read the first lines again. In her present mindset with the emptiness gone, she felt the awakened love and appreciation for her surroundings, and the life and living it offered her. She whispered a prayer of appreciation for all He'd made and His daily artistry. Her eyes welled as she thanked Him for removing the loneliness and replacing it with good friends, even a big brother. With brimming eyes she remembered the casual way she and Matt agreed to adopt each other, but she knew from his prayer that he took the agreement seriously, and since then cared about her like a brother. Yes, God. You are my provider.

On a whim she kissed her finger and pressed it to the last stone.

She spent the remainder of the afternoon reading and relaxing, getting back to the apartment in plenty of time to get ready for dinner. Ethan knocked on her door at 5:45 and they drove to Mac's home. It was several houses down from Vicky's, also on the shore of the inlet. While large it didn't have the mansion-like presence of Vicky's, but more ordinary. He kept the grounds natural sand and a number of trees between the house and street provided shade and privacy.

A woman answered the door and greeted them. She introduced herself as Virginia the housekeeper, and took them out back where Mac was sitting on the deck under an umbrella.

He warmly greeted them, inviting them to sit. Virginia brought out iced tea and said the dinner would be served in 15 minutes. They asked how he was feeling and he said he felt stronger every day. Jules thought he did look less tired and was glad this dinner wouldn't tap him out.

Ethan and Mac talked about the collection of Jet Skis and kayaks on his beach. He'd bought them for when Celeste's children visited, but they didn't get much use these days, he said.

Virginia called them to dinner and checked if there was anything else Mac needed. He thanked her, and as she left she reminded him the nurse would be stopping by around 9:00 to check in on him.

They had an enjoyable meal together as Ethan talked about what he'd been up to since leaving Edisto, and Jules told a bit of her life since her grammy passed away. After dinner Mac asked if Jules would get the dessert tray out of the fridge and bring it out to the deck. When she arrived with plates of peaches and whipped cream, she found the two men settled at a large tiled table with a photo album, a small jewellery box and a short stack of letters. Mac glanced up at her from under heavy brows, then looked down at the things on the table.

"Thank you, Jules. Come sit beside me."

She looked at Ethan to silently ask him if he knew what Mac intended to show her. He stood and as he took the tray from her, he whispered, "It's okay, Jules. Mac is a man of truth." He set the tray on the table and pulled out a chair for her. He rested his hand briefly on her shoulder before sitting down.

Mac pushed his dessert aside and took her hand. "I would like to show you some things of your grandmother's. She and I grew up together. I don't suppose you knew that."

"No."

He opened the photo album to the back and pulled out several loose photos. He gave her a four-picture strip taken from a photo booth. It was of her grammy and Mac when they were in their late teens. Mac had long wavy hair and her grammy's hair was long and straight. They looked like a pair of hippies, together and happy.

"You and Grammy dated?"

"Yes, for over a year."

He gave her another picture of her grammy in a bikini in the waves. Then another one of the two of them dressed up. Jules gasped. "Grammy had one just like this in her drawer. I rescued it before Dad sold all of her things."

"Peggy and I were in love. I asked her to marry me."

"But you didn't get married?"

"No. Her parents were opposed to her marrying me. But we were in love and Peggy was determined. It was the summer of '63. We spent all summer together and by early August Peggy told me she was pregnant. We decided to run away and elope on Labour Day weekend. I told her every day, 'Margaret Ellen Williams, Labour Day long weekend I will make you my wife.' I thought I'd have earned enough money by then to get us set up in a little apartment. A week before the end of August, her parents took her and moved out west. Just before they left she called me to tell me they found out about her pregnancy and were taking her away. She promised to send me a letter or call me to let me know where I could find her. Again I promised her, 'Margaret Ellen Williams, I will come get you on the Labour Day long weekend and make you my wife.'

"I waited and waited, but no letter ever came or phone call ever made. Other than knowing they went out west, I had no idea where she was or how to find her. And no one in town knew where they were, or at least no one was willing to tell me.

"The following year I decided to go to university and got my degree in business. I eventually met and married Nancy. We were happy, but Peggy always held a very special place in my heart. Nancy and I were never able to have any children and I always wondered what became of Peggy and our child."

Jules looked at him a little puzzled. "I thought Celeste was your daughter."

"No, we fostered Celeste. We loved her as our own, but we were never able to adopt her. Her natural father would not sign the papers.

"Anyway, years later Peggy returned to Edisto with your father, our son. I found out her parents had paid Ted Morgan, a young man from a well-respected family, to marry her and give her child his name. It was a loveless marriage. He was in it for the money. He had no love for a child not his own, nor any interest in Peggy. He finally left them for another, more wealthy woman. When Peggy's parents passed away, she inherited a small fortune and decided to move back to Edisto with your father.

"At the time I was married and remained loyal to Nancy, but when my wife was taken with cancer, I tried to start a relationship with Peggy again. I still loved her deeply. She flat out refused. I wanted to be a part of both her and our son's life, but she said the past was best left in the past. Your father was in his midteens by then and wanted nothing to do with anyone in Edisto. Although he was my son, he acted more like the man who gave him his name than either Peggy or me.

"Every year on Labour Day, I would stop by Peggy's house with flowers and a ring to propose to her. She never accepted, but eventually she'd occasionally go for dinner with me. And because Peggy was a good friend to Sandra, and Greg and I were sailing buddies, we would see each other at all the Thomas family holiday dinners.

"While you were here for the summer, she wouldn't let me come over at all and would not let me meet you, but she did give me a copy of every one of your school photos." He handed her a stack of pictures. She shuffled through the worn images seeing the passage of time from a little girl to a teen. She set them down and looked over the entire collection.

He watched her for a moment. "While I watched you from afar and enjoyed seeing you grow up, it broke my heart to not know you. On your 12th birthday I gave Peggy a key to a safety deposit box with a copy of my will inside. I've not changed it since.

"I've made some excellent investments, and very few bad ones, and as a result I have done well for myself. I set up Celeste in a beautiful home and gave her a large trust fund. You, my natural granddaughter, are still the sole benefactor of all I have and own. At the time, I explained to Peggy she was not named in my will because I wanted my estate to go to you, not your father. Based on how he handled Peggy's estate, I think it was a good decision."

He reached for her hands and held them a long moment. He took a deep breath. "Jules, I have loved you your whole life. You are my flesh and blood."

She looked at him with tears spilling down her cheeks. She gulped. "I never knew."

"I know."

He waited.

Taking rapid breaths, holding back her sobs, she looked down at her hands. "I never knew my grandparents."

"I pray you will accept me as family. I thank God He has brought you back into my life. I believe He weaved our lives so you would be here to step into my business and we could finally meet."

"This is a lot to take in." She stood up and hugged him. "Give me some time. It's all a bit overwhelming." Then she left the two men sitting on the deck.

Mac looked out at the ocean with a lone tear rolling down his cheek.

Ethan glanced into the house to see where Jules was heading, then leaned forward and rested his hand on Mac's arm. "I think it'll be okay, Mac. What you said was good. It's time it was said. Give her a bit of time. I think she's been very lonely for family and it might be difficult to hear she's had someone who cared about her all along."

Mac nodded. He picked up the letters and gave them to Ethan. "If you think it'll help or she'd be interested, these are all the letters Peggy ever gave me. I've saved them all these years. They are hers, if she wants. Go look after her now and thank you for bringing her. I hope you're right about having the truth out."

"Will you be okay out here?"

"Yes. I'll rest awhile. The nurse will be here soon enough. Go, go. Take care of her for me, my boy."

He took the letters and tucked them into his inside jacket pocket, grabbed a few napkins and headed back into the house. Jules was no-where to be found. He opened the front door and found her waiting on the front steps. He sat beside her and gave her the napkins. "You okay?"

She nodded and blew her nose. "Do you mind taking me home?"

"Sure." He took her hand and they walked to the truck. He opened the door and let her in. He looked back at the house and whispered a prayer. "Oh Lord, help both of these people overcome the pain of past secrets and finally find the love each of them has to offer the other. And give me the right words to say to Jules."

130

She was quiet for the short drive and he left her to her thoughts. He pulled into the driveway and shut off the engine. They sat quietly for a minute. She looked out the window and he looked at her. He knew the power of silence and gave her space to think. He rested his arm on the seat back and waited.

"It's a lot to take in."

"Yes, I imagine so."

"I'm not sure what I think."

"Take your time. Pray about it. When my wife left me, I discovered God could bring me to a calm and peaceful place where I could think things through. "

"Yeah, I guess you've been through some tough times."

"God's been with me the whole way and He's with you now. Do you want me to pray with you?"

With a new batch of tears welling up, she nodded.

He took her hand. "Our loving heavenly father, thank you for coming into Jules' life. As the author and finisher, you know the start, the middle and the end of our lives. You have prescribed the paths of our lives to bring about your good works. Jules comes to you now feeling a little lost and overwhelmed. We know you work all things out for good for those of us who put our trust in you. We renew our commitment to trust you and ask for your wisdom and direction. Please bring peace to Jules as you help her work through how she's feeling. Quiet her heart and mind, and give her a good night's sleep.

"We also bring Mac before you. Be with him tonight and encourage him. Thank you for all your provision and blessings. In the name of Jesus who died that we might live and live more abundantly, amen."

"Thanks, Ethan."

"Can I walk you to your door, Miss Morgan?"

She laughed, wiped her eyes and blew her nose with the last of the napkins. "If you don't mind being seen with an old wreck."

"A beautiful old wreck."

"You're blind."

"Not so much." He got out and opened her door. Offering her his hand he helped her out. They climbed the steps to the veranda. At her door she turned and hugged him. "Thank you, Ethan. I'm glad you were there this evening."

"You're welcome."

When she stepped back he asked if she was up for a sail on the *Dark Secret* the next day, and they made arrangements to meet at the yacht club at noon.

Tuesday, June 27

Yes, this is a week of big things. Mac says he's my grandfather. Could it be true? Do I actually have family that cares about me?

Quite a revelation, if it's true. I suppose it's possible. Obviously Mac and Grammy were in love. But how can I know for sure Dad is Mac's son? They don't seem alike at all. And it's not what I'd come to believe about my family. Not that my family means much to me. I never knew Mom's parents or Grammy's husband. Grammy was the only good thing in my life.

Then again, Dad isn't much like Grammy. I guess it's possible, but how can I know for sure? Maybe a paternity test, or whatever they call it when checking for a grandparent relationship.

He is a very sweet and gentle man. I would be thrilled if he really is my grandpa. That sounds weird. If he is my grandfather, I'll have to think of some other name. Grampie? No. I'll need to think more about this – about how to figure out if this is true and what I could call him. Oh God, are you giving me a real and loving relative? Almost too good to be true. Please, don't let this be a teaser. I don't want to let my heart get involved if it's not real.

Surprisingly, I think I'm okay with this. I'm kind of proud of myself for stepping away and taking my time. I didn't just slobber all over Mac, grateful that someone, anyone, said they loved me. Good for me. Maybe I do have some of Grammy's strength. Certainly God's strength. Thank you, Jesus.

Once I know for sure, then I can let my emotions go. Until then, I am strong.

And I'm going sailing tomorrow!

Thank you for everything, God.

My word for today is Revelation.

Chapter 18 | Affirmation

Wednesday, June 28

The next day Jules finished work midmorning. She had over an hour before she was to meet Ethan and decided to take a walk down the beach. She needed a bit of time to think over all Mac had said.

She noted a good wind coming from the southeast and thought it should make for a good sail. Without thinking where she was going, she found herself heading for the weeping dune and was excited to find two new stones. The first one said, "My eyes transfixed with the ever-changing palette in the sky," and the second one, "I watch the artist paint the transition from day to night." She remembered last time thinking the author had changed direction, but noticed these two lines were something of a follow-up to her favourite first line, "The One who paints in colour and clouds." She wondered if this was the new pattern for the next lines.

She considered the new lines and felt they resonated. *I've contemplated God and His provision, and I'm watching Him change my world from night to day. He's changing the colours in my life, and making it something beautiful.*

She felt a kinship with the author. She thought it amazing how he captured the unthought words of her heart and then left them here for her to discover.

She hurried back to the apartment and quickly changed for the boat. As she pulled into the parking lot she saw Ethan leaning against his truck with a backpack on his shoulder. He wore a midblue blue tank top that brought his blue eyes to life when he looked up at her. *Is it me or do colours just seem brighter and more beautiful today?* She pulled in beside him and he opened her door for her. "I hope I'm not late."

"No, not at all. In fact, you're a few minutes early. How are you today?"

"Well, I'm ready for Edisto's famous international sailing genius to take me on an exciting sail."

Laughing, he said, "Okay, your wish is my command. Let's go see what the *Dark Secret* can do."

Ethan steered the boat out of the dock, and gave the wheel to Jules to steer them along the river and out to the inlet while he took the covers off the sails. As they entered the bay, he shut off the engine and hoisted the main and jib sails. He pointed where she needed to steer and tightened the sheets to a close reach. The sails filled and the vessel took off across the waves.

He stood beside her at the helm. She looked at him with a contented smile. He got out an electronic device that looked like a TV remote with a large screen. Turning it on and setting it up he explained, it was a GPS device to measure their location and speed. He looked at the sails, made a couple of adjustments to the sheets and read the GPS again.

They had travelled to the middle of the inlet. Ethan said, "Okay, captain. Do you remember how to call a tack?"

"I do."

"Then let's turn to port and take her out to sea." He moved to the port side ready to release the sheet. "Ready, captain."

"Helms alee!" She spun the wheel and turned them through the wind, pointing the vessel straight out to sea. Ethan adjusted the sails and checked the GPS. She checked the reading as he made more adjustments to the direction and sails. When he cinched the sheet to the cleat, she called out the new speed.

He stood beside her again, and said, "She should be a bit faster, but those sails are a bit small and they look old and stretched. They probably should be replaced." He looked ahead on either side of the sails for vessels that could cross their path. "Let's stay on this tack and get well out into open waters, then we'll take her on a close-hauled tack." Resting his arm around her shoulders, he said, "I promised you an exciting ride. Close hauled is the one that heels the boat on its side and makes you laugh. Then we'll take her beam reach. That should be her fastest.

He put the boat through the different points of sail, teaching her more sailing lingo. He then set sail inland.

When they got near the shore, he dropped the sails and taught her how to set anchor. "I brought some stuff in my pack, if you want to open the front and dig it out." She pulled out a bag of cookies, a box of crackers, a block of cheese and a knife. As he hopped off the cabin into the cockpit, he said, "I didn't say it was fancy." He took a seat beside her.

They quietly ate a couple of crackers. Pointing to his left shoulder blade, she said, "I never expected a minister to have tats. What are they?"

Pulling his tank top aside to expose all of them, he said, "I got them when I was in racing. There's one for the first time I won each race."

"You have the Olympic rings!"

"Yeah. First in Finn class and second in Star class."

"That's amazing. I've never known an Olympic champion. Do you miss racing?"

"I still love sailing, but no, I don't miss racing." She knew there had to be a very dramatic story to make him quit racing and not miss it. Maybe one day he'd tell her.

After a long pause she said, "Do you know Mac well?

"About as well as I knew Auntie Peggy."

"Tell me about him."

"What would you like to know?"

"What kind of man is he?

"He's a good man. He's honest, ethical and kindhearted. It might've been a bit hard to tell yesterday, but he laughs easily and enjoys life."

She thought for a long moment. "If what he said is true, I wonder why Grammy never told me."

He looked at her while he made a decision, then got up, opened the side pocket of his pack and pulled out the letters Mac had given him. He sat back down beside her and gave them to her. "Mac said these were all the letters Aunt Peggy wrote to him. He wanted you to have them."

"Have you read them?"

"No."

She took them and checked the front of each envelope. He leaned back, stretched his arms out on the deck rails and closed his eyes to give her time. He heard her open an envelope and the papers inside. She slid back on the seat beside him, leaned her head on his shoulder and quietly read the first one.

He heard it go back in the envelope and waited for her to comment, but instead he heard her open the next one. She read through every one.

"It's true. She was in love with him. And she talked very lovingly of her pregnancy and the love child they shared. These last ones were written in August of 1963 and my dad was born in early March of '64. I'm really his granddaughter."

"Yes."

"Did you know?"

He hesitated, not knowing how she would take the answer. He breathed a quick prayer and sat up. "Yes. One Christmas dinner when I was a kid, Mac came over, well on his way to a good drunk. Aunt Peggy always made holiday dinners with Mom. Frank wasn't there.

He never came to any of our dinners. He really wanted nothing to do with life in Edisto.

"Anyway, Mac asked Aunt Peggy to marry him at the dinner table in front of all of us. He stood up and proposed a toast to the only woman to steal his heart. Aunt Peggy tried to shush him up, but he would have none of it. At first, we kids thought it was funny, but Mom hushed us up. He refused to be quiet. Finally he said, 'Margaret Ellen Williams, I promised to come get you on the Labour Day long weekend and make you my wife and I'd like to keep my promise. It's time Frank lived with his real father.'"

"Silence reigned the table as we all absorbed what Mac had just said. Mom looked down. Matt, Cass and I just stared at Mac and Aunt Peggy. Dad tried to get Mac to sit down.

Mac refused. "I'm waiting, woman."

Finally Aunt Peggy stood up, and said, "I love you, you old fool, but I cannot marry you. Now sit down and let's eat."

Jules laughed. "That sounds like Grammy."

"Mom and Dad moved the conversation in another direction, and afterward Dad informed each one of us kids that if we ever told a soul about what we'd heard, we would regret it and our behinds would pay to an inch of our lives. I've never breathed a word to anyone outside the family. Jules, I'm sorry, but I couldn't tell you because it wasn't my secret to tell. But I'm glad you know the truth."

"So who all knows?"

"Me, Mom and Dad, Cass and Matt were the only ones there. Somewhere along the line Ryan figured it out, and of course Mac's brother Alistair knows. Mac also said Celeste has known all along that he had a son and granddaughter, but I'm not sure she knew who. She probably does now, though."

After a long time Jules said, "I have a grandfather. He's a good man. He says he loves me and always has. And he's an accountant. I guess that runs in the family."

Smiling at her thought process, he said, "I guess so. From what I know of both of you, I don't think the apple has fallen far from the tree. I see a lot of both Mac and Aunt Peggy in you."

"I have a grandfather."

"Yes, you do."

"And he loves me."

"Yes, he does."

"I think I like that."

"I think Mac will be glad to hear it." She leaned back on his shoulder and they sat quietly, rocking in the waves. Ethan thought about what God told him just a few days earlier. Soon there would come a day when Jules would need him and he needed to be ready to fulfill the role God asked of him. With Jules tucked in his arm, he knew this was the time God had spoken of, and thanked Him for His wisdom and grace.

Before leaving the sheltered inlet, he pulled out a mask, snorkel and fins from his pack. He wanted a look at the hull. After a couple of dives, he climbed back onboard.

"Everything okay?"

"It could use a good scraping. There's a fair amount of slime and barnacles. That would certainly affect the speed at the lower knots. And it explains why she heels a lot more than she should."

When they got back to dock, Ethan had a bit of business with a few men at the club and invited Jules to stay for awhile. Jules thought it best she leave him to his business and went home. She leaned in and kissed his cheek. "Thanks for a great afternoon. I appreciate you honestly telling me about the past."

"You're welcome." He watched her go for a moment, then went into the clubhouse.

While making her dinner she heard Ethan's truck pull in. Two doors slammed closed and she heard Ethan talking with another man as they went into Cass' house.

She enjoyed a leisurely dinner, engrossed in a critically exciting part of one of her books. Before she realized an hour and a half had slipped by. She quickly cleaned up the dishes and went for a walk along the beach. She remembered her wonderful discovery at the weeping dunes that morning, and decided to stop in and read them again. She was pleasantly surprised to discover two more stones. "I stand arms outstretched to feel your caressing wind." Then, "And feel your breath whispering in my ear." *Yes, it followed the new pattern, referencing back to the earlier line about God drawing out the paths for the wind to follow. It's like Mac had said. God directed their paths to cross. I too felt your caressing wind and now it's time I listen for your whisper in my ear. Lord, what should I do about Mac? Please tell me and I promise to try to listen.*

Then thinking about the author, she knew he was a sailor and understood his feeling for the caressing wind. Although she knew it was a remote possibility, considering all the people who lived in Edisto Beach, she wondered again if it could be Ethan. *No, it can't be. The author had placed these two new stones sometime after she had been here midmorning, and I met Ethan at the marina immediately after. Then we were together all afternoon, and I heard him come home and go inside with someone. And his truck was still in the driveway when I came down here. I don't think he's had a chance to come down here.*

She felt a little disappointed that it couldn't be Ethan. She was back to square one to figure out who it was.

Climbing into bed she looked at her grammy's letters on the night stand.

Wednesday, June 28

I have all the proof I need. My hopes have been affirmed. Mac is my grandfather. I could never have imagined such a thing. He's a sweet man, and to think he loves me and has for such a long time. It's kind of weird to discover someone has loved me dearly and deeply from afar and I never knew. Thank you, God, for bringing me here to find you, an adopted brother and my grandfather.

Ethan said he sees both Mac and Grammy in me. My perception of my heritage just improved significantly today. Mac is a man I can be proud to say is my grandfather. Maybe all good traits skip a generation.

I need to let Mac know as soon as possible I've thought about it and would like to get to know him. When I think about him, warmth fills my chest. I can't wait to tell him and build a friendship with him. Maybe we can have the kind of thing I see with Ethan and Cass and their parents. Thank you, God. for giving me a loving grandfather and a good family example to follow.

I'm a little scared Mac will be disappointed in me once he gets to know me. Now that I've been given family, I'm readying myself to run away. I need to stop letting these negative thoughts take hold. I am Jules. I am strong.

My word for today is Affirmation.

Chapter 19 | Reconciliation

Thursday, June 29

After work on Thursday morning, Jules dropped in on Mac. He opened the door and smiled when he saw her. "My girl, come on in. Would you like a glass of sweet tea?"

They went to the kitchen while he poured their drinks, then led her to the back sitting room overlooking the water.

"It looks like a storm is getting ready to blow in."

He waited for her to settle into the large chair across from him. "I guess I gave you a lot to think about."

"Yes. Ethan gave me Grammy's letters. I can tell she really loved you. And it's pretty clear that you're my grandfather."

"Yes." He sat back in his seat, resting his hand thoughtfully on his mouth.

"Ethan tells me you proposed to Grammy one Christmas dinner and she said she could never marry you. Why not?"

"That's true. I didn't find out her reason for many years. Then one summer just after you left to go back home, she came over to see me. I thought she'd come to finally accept, but that was not to be. I guess it was more of a pre-emptive strike. I think she wanted me to stop coming over every Labour Day and proposing marriage.

"We sat right out there on the deck. She said she regretted letting her parents take her away and bully her into a loveless marriage. She sent me a letter, but because I never got it, we figure her parents got a hold of it somehow or it coincidentally got lost in the mail. I never answered and she thought I had changed my mind. She reluctantly agreed to marry her parents' choice.

"Ted was pretty rough on both her and your dad. He left her unable to have any more children, and tormented your father, turning him into a disillusioned and frustrated boy. Frank coped by shutting off his feelings and simply not caring about anyone. It hurt Peggy deeply that you suffered because of Frank's lack. I know she tried to pour love into your life every summer.

"Anyway, she said she was damaged goods and felt enormous guilt that she'd allowed our son, our love child, to be damaged as well. She said she didn't feel worthy to be a wife to anyone, let alone me. Before I could say anything, she got up and left.

"So a couple of days later, on Labour Day, I got on my best suit, took the ring with some flowers and went over to her place to propose. She opened the door and knew why I was there. Again, she said she wasn't worthy of my love. I said it didn't matter what she thought about her past. I loved her right there, right then, and wanted to marry her. She told me she loved me too, more than I could imagine, but she just couldn't. She closed the door and I stood there a long time listening to her weep. I knocked and called, but she wouldn't answer. The house became silent. I went home.

"That was the last Labour Day she had on this earth. She passed away the following spring. I was on vacation when you and your father came to finalize her estate and I never saw you again until you came here the other day." He looked at her a long moment. "You remind me a lot of my sweet Peggy. And just as much as I loved my Peggy, I love you, my girl."

She thought about her grandmother not feeling worthy and shutting him out. "I can understand not feeling worthy and shutting down."

Looking at her closely to read what she was really saying, he said, "She was wrong, you know. I didn't care about her past. I loved her the person, not her past experiences."

She silently nodded and looked out the windows. "Jules, don't you walk the same path as Peggy. Bad things happen to everyone. Cutting out your heart, denying yourself life with the living, and accepting memories as your future is wrong. God takes all the wrong that we've done and throws it into the sea of forgetfulness. He does this because He wants to give us today and a future of His abundance. If you keep resurrecting the past, you will live in the past and not walk in the blessings He has planned for you. Her mistake wasn't in having a bad experience, but in living her life in that past. Now I don't know much about you and your past, but I believe your coming to Edisto and back into my life is a part of God's provision for you and me. I see this as a resetting of your life and your direction. You have a choice, just like Peggy did. Peggy chose the past and lost out on the blessing of the future. I think you have the same choice to make. And I think you are too young to live in the past."

She walked to the windows. "I know. I'm trying really hard to learn a new way of life, but I don't think I know how to not let the pain of the past rise up and dictate my future. There are times when I'm playing on the water that I forget everything, but then I see a family and it sweeps in again. It's easy to say, 'Let go and move on,' but pain and loneliness are all I've known and it's hard to trust that it could be any different today or tomorrow. I feel like I've been in the darkness so long I don't know how to stay in the light. My past has been filled with crying and wailing in the darkness, but it's so dark, it absorbed my cries and no one heard."

He stood up and moved beside her to look out over the sea and the incoming storm. "You walk with the Creator of the universe, the King of life, the One that brings a new day and new blessings. God is bigger than the vastness of the universe, and He loves and cares about you. He has brought you out of darkness. He holds you in His hand where life and love flourish. Are you going to let your past without God stop you from enjoying all He wants to give you?"

She smiled through her tears at her error in thinking and the clarity Mac brought to her muddled view. "When you put it that way, I guess not."

He gave her a hug. "I wish I knew about you sooner – Mac. I think I missed out on a lot of your wisdom. By the way, calling you Mac doesn't sound right anymore. Now I don't know what to call you."

"Whatever you're comfortable with."

"It might take me a bit of time to get to know you. You've known me and about me for almost three decades. It'll take time for me to catch up."

"Well, you can take your time, but keep in mind I'm over 70 and I've had a heart attack. I don't have decades left."

Jules smiled at his cheeky comment. "You're not so old, and it won't take me decades. I've planned to spend the summer here, so I can come over often and we can get to know each other. Say, what is your first name? I don't think I've heard anyone call you by it."

"I'm Robert Declan MacKenzie. Somewhere along the line I picked up the nickname Mac and it stuck. I don't think anyone knows my first name anymore."

"Declan. I like it. But that's Irish, isn't it?"

"Yes. MacKenzie is Gaelic and Robert has a fine Scottish history, but our family had deep ties with the Irish."

"Well, Robert Declan MacKenzie, how would you like it if I called you Poppa? You don't seem much like a Grampie."

"I like Poppa. Thank you, Jules."

They chatted for a couple of hours about both their lives, and when she saw he was getting tired, she left him with a warm hug and kiss on the cheek. "Bye, my poppa."

"Bye my wee girl. Come by anytime." She drove home with her heart singing, and decided to spend the remainder of the afternoon down on the beach before the storm blew in.

As usual, she went to the weeping dune to check for new stones, not expecting anything. But there were another two stones. "I consider the morning, then look to the ocean to decipher the day's inclination." And, "And then I seek your inclination for my day." *Oh, it must be someone who came down here this morning.* She read them a couple of times. They made more sense when she read the related earlier line, "The One who created the ocean as a mirror reflecting the mood of the day." She liked the thought that he came here this morning to spend time with God, and just as one would look over the ocean and sky to see what the day would bring, he looked to the Lord to prepare him for what his day would bring.

I know Grammy spent time with God in the evenings and she had started to read her Bible every night before going to bed, but I wonder if it wasn't better to start her day with Him rather than end it. Then I'd be ready for what my day would bring. If this author is right, the day's inclination is stormy. Thankfully, things went well with Poppa. I may have averted my storm. Then she heard it. The wind blew through the grasses just right, and she heard the low moan. She looked to the horizon at the approaching storm.

She remembered it'd been a stormy day when she first heard the weeping dune. It'd not been a good day as she said goodbye to her Grammy's home and love. Here she was so many years later with another approaching storm. Only this time she wasn't losing a grandmother, but gaining a grandfather who wanted to welcome her into his family. She was letting go of her past in exchange for a bright future with God. She thought about how life had cycled back to a storm and a weeping dune. She sat for a long time in the valley of the dune, listening to the lonesome cadence of the rise and fall of its song. It didn't seem so sad this time.

She looked at the sky and knew they were in for a stormy night. She finally got up and slowly made her way home, thinking about Mac, her new life, the weeping dune and how the poem seemed to be written for her. As she neared her driveway, a man got out of a car and her heart sank. *A stormy night indeed.*

An hour earlier a car pulled into Cass' driveway. A stranger got

147

out and impatiently knocked on her front door. When Cass answered he demanded to see Juleena. She told him she wasn't staying there, but if he wanted to leave a message, she would get it to her. He yelled Juleena's name, but no one answered.

"I told you, she's not staying here."

"I know she's here. And you can't stop me from talking to her."

"She's not and you won't be standing on my veranda yelling at no one." She closed the door and watched as this man left the porch to sit in his car. It looked like he had no intention of leaving and left her a little nervous. Ryan had to return to Atlanta for a couple of days and she felt a little vulnerable. She was about to call Ethan when she saw him pull into the driveway.

Ethan knocked on the car window and asked if he could help.

The man rolled down his window. "Yes, tell me where Juleena is. Your wife won't tell me."

Ethan looked up and saw Cass looking out the window. "She's not my wife and she's right, Jules isn't here, but I can let her know you were looking for her."

"No, I know this is where she is. I'll wait until you send her out," he said and rolled up his window.

Ethan busied himself outside sorting his tools in the storage shed. He heard the car door open and poked his head out to see Jules coming up the street.

The man said, "I knew you were here."

"What are you doing here?"

"We need to talk."

"Anders, I told you, it's over. There's nothing to talk about." Hearing the name Anders, Ethan kept his eye on their exchange.

Anders grabbed her arm. "It's not over until I say it's over. Now stop being so childish and come home."

She pulled back, but his grip was too tight. "Anders, let go." Ethan stepped out to stop things from escalating. "Hey man, dial it back. Be civil or leave." Anders looked at him and violently released her arm.

"Get in the car, Juleena."

"I already told you, I'm taking another direction in my life."

"What? You've joined some kind of Christian cult? You think they will treat you any better?"

"No, I haven't joined a cult. I've accepted Jesus as my Lord."

"Whatever. Come on, Juleena. Get in the car. Time to leave this hick town and all its hick ideas."

"I won't. But I think you should leave."

"Enough of this nonsense. I'm not going to tell you again. Get in the car." He reached out to grab her again and Ethan stepped between them, holding Anders away from Jules.

"Ease back, man. You need to cool down."

"And who are you? This is none of your business." Shoving Ethan, he leaned toward Jules, pointing at Ethan. "Is this your new sucker? Gonna rope this one in, then leave him high and dry too?"

Ethan moved between them again. "I think you need to leave."

Anders pushed Ethan, pointed at him and growled, "You best stay out of my way. I'm here to talk to Juleena, not you."

Again, Ethan stepped between them, holding Anders back. "You're a little too hot for conversation. It's best you leave before you go too far."

Jules said, "This isn't talking. You're expecting me to cow to your demands. Well, I'm not going to. My life is on a different path now. I'm not going back to New York. And I'm certainly not going back to you. Best you leave. We have nothing more to talk about, Anders. You ended it when you took a swing at me."

"I never hit you."

"Not for lack of trying."

"If you don't come with me now, you'd better get your stuff out of my apartment before Sunday when I'm back, or I'll throw it out."

He shoved Ethan one more time, then stormed to his car. Before getting in he emphatically pointed at Jules. "You'll regret this. This hick will never give you what I can." He threw it into gear and nearly drove over them to get back onto the street, then peeled out. Jules thought, *No one will ever have the chance to give me what you offer ever again.*

Ethan turned to Jules. "You okay?"

"Surprisingly, yes. But it looks like I need to go to New York to get my things."

"I don't think you should go alone. He could be there waiting for you. How about I go with you? He won't try anything with me there."

Matt drove in while they were talking in the driveway. He sensed the serious nature of the conversation. "What's up?" Ethan looked at the menacing sky and suggested they go inside. Cass was waiting with a hot tea for Jules. Ethan explained to Matt and Cass what had happened in the driveway.

"Jules needs to go to New York and get her things out of the apartment by Sunday. I'm going to go with her. I don't think she should go alone."

Matt casually hung his arm around Jules. "Sounds like this might be a job for a big brother. Ethan, want some company?"

"Anders definitely wouldn't try anything with the two of us there."

Jules said, "I don't think he'll be there. He said he wouldn't be back until Sunday. So if I go before then, he won't be there."

Matt said, "I don't think you should risk it. Ethan and I will go with you."

"I don't know what I'm going to do with my stuff when we get it. At the end of August I'll be homeless. In the meantime I guess I could it put in storage somewhere."

Ethan said, "Don't worry about being homeless. None of us is about to let you live on the streets. How much stuff do you have?"

She thought for a moment. "My clothes, books, a few paintings, a small chest that I keep all my sentimental things in. It has the only things I have of Grammy. I want that for sure. Then there's a small handcrafted jewellery box, some things in the bathroom and a few knickknacks. And my vehicle. It's not much, I guess."

"I don't think you need a storage unit. For the few boxes, why don't you store them at my house? I'm still renovating it, so there's lots of room there. It'll give you time to sort out what you're going to do come the fall."

"Okay thanks, you guys. I don't mean to be a bother."

Matt said, "I wouldn't be much of a brother if I let you deal with this on your own. Besides, Ethan and I are overdue for a road trip. Haven't done that since high school."

Ethan said, "What kind of car do you have?"

"It's a Jeep Wrangler. We really only used it on weekends."

"Does it have a trailer hitch?"

"Yeah, it came with one. Why?"

"We could fly in and rent a small trailer we can tow behind the Jeep to carry all your things. That would be the quickest way to get your belongings and it wouldn't require that we drive up in one car and back in two."

Matt said, "That sounds like a plan. What do you think, Jules? Fly in Saturday morning. It wouldn't take long to pack and get on the road. We could be back by midnight, probably. It'll be a long day, but we'd have three drivers."

"It sounds good. Thank you, everyone. Thanks, Ethan, for standing with me in front of Anders. I'm sure he would have gotten physically violent if you weren't there."

"Yeah, I think it's pretty likely. That's what the men of Carolina do for our ladies."

That evening she called Susan to find out how Anders could have figured out her location. Susan told her she had no contact with him since picking up her things, but she would follow up at work to see if someone there told him.

Thursday, June 29

A stormy day.

As the stone poet writes, I seek your inclination every day, God, and look where you have brought me! I am reconciled – to you, to my poppa, to my home and my people!

I am still struggling with my past. All I have ever known is a lonely desperation, always on the verge of emotional breakdown. I've cried for love in the vast emptiness and it just absorbed my pleas. The silence there was deafening. It offered no relief. I've seen the life in the light of you, but I don't know how to let go of the past and live in your present and your future for me. Please show me how to forget – show me how to let go of the dead things of the past.

What did Poppa say? You hold me in your hand where life and love flourish. Am I going to let my past without you stop me from enjoying all that you want to give me? The answer is I don't want to, but I need you to show me how to let go of such fresh memories. Poppa says they need to become history – just facts of the past with no emotional impact. I need to figure out how to move on.

Well today, the tempest came and left, and I didn't get soaked. Like a tornado Anders blew in, expecting to suck me into his chaos again, but I stood my ground and none of his verbal jabs landed. Thank you, Jesus, that his power over me, his power to cripple and hurt me, is gone. I don't need him.

I have God, and I have a poppa who loves me, I have a brother and I have a friend willing to stand by me.

I am not alone. I am reconciled to all you have to offer in Edisto.

Oh, I can't thank you enough, Jesus. Don't let me forget all you are giving me. Help me stand strong like they do. Show me the way to that kind of strength.

My word for today is Reconciliation.

Chapter 20 | Freedom

Saturday, July 1

Cass drove them into Charleston at 3:30 a.m. to catch the first flight out. Matt sat across the aisle, letting Ethan and Jules have the two seats together. Jules had been quiet since starting out, and sat staring out the window. "Are you worried?" Ethan asked.

"No, not really. Just thinking about what to do in the fall."

"What are your options?"

"My company is in New York City, but we work all over so, I think I could really be anywhere along the eastern coast. I don't want to be in New York anymore."

He hoped she'd say she wanted to move to Edisto and felt a little disappointed she didn't mention it. Then he wondered what his future actually held. He wasn't even sure he'd be there. And he'd promised Matt to not do anything to hurt Jules. *Perhaps I'd misinterpreted what God meant when He told me He'd set Jules on my path.*

Jules interrupted his thoughts. "I know I haven't spent much time in Edisto, but I really like it there. And now I've found I've got family there. I've been thinking maybe I could move there. It's not too far to Charleston for when I need to fly out to project sites."

155

Once they landed they took a cab directly to the apartment, and after they found no sign of Anders, Matt drove her Jeep to the rental place to pick up the trailer. When he got back with boxes, Jules was gathering her things and piling them on the table, and Ethan began packing. Matt loaded the filled boxes on the trailer. With the three of them working, it took a couple of hours and they were on the road.

They sang along with the radio, talked and laughed their way through New York and Pennsylvania. It felt like her old college days going on spring break. They took turns at the wheel with the shotgun seat as navigator and conversationalist. The third often napped in the back. They got home just after midnight, all stiff and tired, and were in bed in ten minutes. She had one thought before falling asleep.

I am finally, totally, free!

Chapter 21 | Inspiration

Sunday, July 2

When Jules awoke late the next morning, she decided to lounge in bed awhile and read her Bible for over an hour. Finally she got up and took her breakfast out to the veranda. The honeymoon couple next door left for a day at the beach. She noted Ethan's truck was gone and thought he must have gone to church. The trailer was still hitched to her Jeep. She would need to unload it and get it back to the rental place in Charleston. And with her Jeep here, she wouldn't need the rental car any longer. But she would need Ethan's help with both these things.

Enjoying the quiet that comes with a lazy Sunday, she decided to read on the veranda for awhile. After a few chapters Ethan drove in. "Hey Jules, how are you today?"

"Good, and you?"

"I'm good. Want to unload the trailer and get it back today?"

"I was just thinking about that. Do you think we could take the rental car back at the same time?"

"Sure. When do you want to head over to my house to unload the trailer?"

"Anytime you're ready."

"Okay, let's go now."

Ethan drove her Jeep and she followed in her rental car. He pulled into an small, old cottage on the oceanside waterfront. It was a large property and a beautiful location, but she could see the place needed some attention. He showed her around and talked about all the changes and improvements he had planned. He had opened up the back of the home into one large room. He pointed to a stack of windows on the floor and said he planned on replacing the back wall with floor-to-ceiling windows that could be rolled to the sides, opening the room to the ocean breezes. He talked of the addition to the side he had building permits for to add a large master bedroom oceanside, a main bath and a couple of spare rooms. She could see the difference already with the work and thought it would be a wonderful place when completed.

It took about half an hour to unload her things. Jules dug through the chest and pulled out her grammy's shoe box to bring with her. They drove the two vehicles to Charleston, getting back midafternoon. Matt, Ryan and Cass were stacking surfboards into Cass' trunk as they pulled into the driveway. Matt said, "Good wind today. You two interested in coming?"

Ethan looked at Jules and she said, "Sounds good to me. I'm pretty stiff from all the driving, but I think I still need an instructor."

Matt said, "Let me get the long board. I'll be glad to help you."

Ethan said, "I'm in too. I'll change and grab my board."

On the way down, Matt suggested Ethan enjoy the waves, and he would spend the afternoon with Jules, if he wanted some time on the good ones. Ethan offered to split his time. He thought after his conversation with his dad that morning, he needed some alone time to clear his head. Ethan, Ryan and Cass headed for the large waves and Matt took Jules back up to the smaller surf. After an hour Ethan came by to see how she was doing and cheered as she rode a wave in to its foamy end. He gave Matt his board and took over with Jules. She had improved quickly, managing to fall only a couple of times.

After an hour they walked back to the truck to find the others hanging out on the beach, waiting for them. They sat down and chatted awhile. Jules thought Ethan seemed a little quiet, but attributed it to fatigue and felt bad he'd spent so much time helping her over the past few days.

When the conversation died down, Ethan asked if they'd all like to go out for dinner. He had something he wanted to talk over with them. After cleaning up from the ocean, they went to Grover's.

Once they had their orders in, Ethan said, "So I had brunch with Dad this morning. He wanted to talk to me about taking over for him at the marina. He thinks if I start offering my services as a sailing instructor, I could start part-time and gradually take on more of the management over time. He's thinking he'd like to semi retire."

"Dad talked to you about his retirement?"

"I don't think he's ready to give up his business just yet, but he's thinking about how to structure things for his retirement. If I don't join him, he said he'll have to decide if he wants to keep the business and try to find someone he trusts to take over the management, or if he should sell it."

"Oh Eth, I know how much he loves that business, but that's a lot of pressure on you," said Cass.

"I don't think he meant it that way, really. I think he's just feeling me out to see if handing it over to me is a possibility. He wants me to be happy and not burdened with a business I don't really want. So I've been thinking it over today and I'm on the fence. One thing I'd like to know is if you'd be interested in the business for yourself, Cass."

Cass glanced at Ryan and reached for his hand. Looking at Ethan she said, "To be honest, Dad asked me about a year ago if I was interested and I told him that I'd think about it – back when you were in Texas. But when we decided to buy the property next door and get it set up for renting, I went back to Dad and turned him down. And now we have another reason. You are the first people we've told. We're expecting."

Ethan went over to Cass, hugged her and kissed her cheek. "Congratulations, Cass. This is fantastic news." He turned and patted Ryan on the back, "Congratulations, Dad."

Matt and Jules followed with their congratulations. Jules asked when she'd be due. "The doctor estimated the middle of January. So you see, I have no interest in taking over Dad's business. It's all yours, if you want it."

"If I want it – that is the question. I don't think I'd be too worked up about the administration and management part, if it only entailed that."

Matt said, "You mentioned instructing? Would that tip the scales for you?"

"Well, that just it. A number of the men at the club have asked for help both with their skills and for advice with their boats. Jules and I took Jim Gallagher's new boat this week to sort out why it's slow and sluggish. And I like helping these guys out, but I don't think I'm much interested in opening a school for beginner tourists." He glanced at Jules, realizing what he'd just said might offend her. "I didn't mean you, Jules."

Matt laughed. "No, she's in a category of her own."

Ryan joined in on the teasing. "What category is that? Really pretty girls?"

Ethan looked at Jules to see how she was doing. She was smirking at the lads' comments. He said, "Really pretty girls that have come back home to Edisto is the category, actually.

"Anyway, I wanted your ideas and thoughts on the viability of something other than buying a raft of Sunfish and teaching a bunch of hormone-distracted teens how to sail on their vacation. I think that would drive me crazy."

Their dinners arrived and it gave them time to think over what Ethan had said. "So? Do you have any thoughts? I'm open to what you think of the fit of me taking over the business, and any ideas you might have."

Ryan said, "I've known you for a number of years and thought you were a bit of an adrenaline junkie. But you surprised me when you gave it all up for the ministry. To be really honest with you, I never quite saw it as a fit for you. The marina makes more sense to me, but really I think this needs to be a question between your heart and mind. If nothing about managing resonates now, I can't see you being very happy five years from now."

"You're right, Ryan. I feel a pull back to the ocean, but not working in the offices all day. I'm really at a crossroads, and I think I can't see the forest for the trees. I wondered if any of you would have some ideas I hadn't considered."

Cass said, "You know I love you being back in town and want you to stay. You're going to be an uncle soon enough and our child would be lucky to have one nearby, but I want you to be finally happy. If sailing does that for you, I think you should find a way to make it work. Could you do renovations part-time and something with sailing the rest of the time?"

"I could, but that doesn't really help Dad to semi retire."

Matt said, "I agree with Ryan. I see you as an adrenaline junkie and think whatever you choose to do has to include feeding your need. And I agree with you. I can't see you happy dealing with the hormone-raging vacationers, as you call them. But you always seem grounded when you've had time on the water. I think you need to find a career path that either has you on the water, or gives you the time and money to get your fix."

Smiling at Matt's analogy, "Yes, my love of the wind and water can feel like an addiction. I did miss it when living in Virginia, Louisiana and Texas. It's made a huge difference in my recovery from my divorce."

There was a long pause while everyone thought and ate their meals. Ethan turned to Jules. "You haven't said much."

"Well, actually, I kind of think I'm not family and haven't known you that long, really."

"And that's why I want to hear what you think. You don't have all my history to taint your thinking."

She looked at him for a moment to consider if she should share what she thought. "I'm not saying I'm right, but I've watched you sail a couple of times and Matt's right. You really seem in your element on the water – like it's where you belong.

"I've watched you with advanced sailors like your dad and Cass and I know what you are like when teaching me. Ethan, you are a natural instructor.

"I understand your shying away from teaching the vacationers, but I suspect it's more related to the fact that you like to invest in people in a meaningful way. And that's probably the part of ministry that you found appealing. The vacationers are here and gone, and you don't see the growth and development. So I think anything that fulfills your need to help people advance and mature would fit the bill for you.

"And as to if there's a way to make this work for both you and your dad, you are a world-class sailor. You love and understand the nuances of each boat. The men here are proud to have had one of their sons on the sailing world stage. I think you could leverage your sailing skill and knowledge, your natural instructional talent, the fame you've earned, and your love for people development to offer services to grow and develop the competent and mature sailors. I would think with your name and reputation as a sailing champion, guys would come from all over to spend a week or two under your instruction, and I think people within reasonable sailing distance would bring their boats to be instructed on the subtleties of their own boat.

"As a marina, could you offer not only the basics for engines, but maybe you could make it a sailing specialty shop too. With your knowledge and contacts, you could follow up on your advice and provide the service, sails, and other equipment that might be hard to find elsewhere. Maybe not stock it, but be able to get it in quickly.

"As to the management and administration, didn't you say your dad considered hiring someone to help out in that area? Could you find someone that you could provide oversight, but they would do the work you find tedious and grinding? You could even bring them on and let your dad help you train them while he shifts into semiretirement.

"Like I said, I really don't know your dad's business and I may be way off the mark on what other sailors would be interested in, but you asked what I think, and I think there is a way to make this work that would satisfy your love of the ocean and provide you the satisfaction of seeing people advance. I think this is an opportunity most rare for a man with a most rare talent."

The table sat silent for a moment. Ethan sat with his arms resting on the table, looked down at his meal slowly shaking his head. Jules thought she may have misread things or stepped over the line. She opened her mouth to apologize when Ethan smiled, then laughed. "You've pegged me, my girl."

Matt said, "Yeah, you nailed him. You're bang on."

Cass said, "You are very intuitive, Jules. I think you are right. Right down the line, I agree with everything you said. Yeah, the men in town all clamour for your time Ethan. And I do think lots of people would be interested in coming and learning from you. Jules is right. You're a fantastic teacher. I think she's hit on something viable. And I bet Dad would love this idea of adding to his operation by providing quality sailing instruction and supplies."

Ethan looked up. "Ryan, what do you think?"

"I think you should listen to your heart. If you can find passion in what you do, you'll be happy for life and I'd like to see you find your passion."

Now grinning, Ethan said, "It does resonate. The more I think about it, the more I think it's a good idea. Thanks, everyone. I was hoping you'd have some good ideas. And Jules, I think you should go into career counselling. You've read me like a book. Thank you for sharing your thoughts."

"You're welcome. You've done so much for me over the last few days. I'm glad if I've helped you." They chatted on for the rest of the meal and well into the evening with marketing and promotional ideas.

Ryan reminded them that Tuesday would be Independence Day and asked if they had plans yet. Matt said he made arrangements for a surprise that would keep them busy most of the day. They bugged him to divulge his secret, but he insisted it was a surprise.

Ryan said he and Cass were going shark fishing on Monday and invited the others along. Jules said she wasn't much into sharks or fishing and passed. Matt decided to join them and Ethan said he had some things to do in the morning and would pass.

Ethan thanked them all again, saying he wanted to pray about it, but thought he would talk it over with his dad in the next day or two.

When they got home Ethan invited Jules for a walk along the beach. They said good evening to the others, then headed down the street. They looked at each other, and Ethan smiled and took her hand. "You're a pretty great gal, you know."

"You're a pretty great guy too."

They walked in a companionable silence for several minutes. Bending down Ethan picked up a piece of rose-coloured glass, edges rounded by the sand and surf. "You don't see pink sea glass too often," and gave it to her.

"It's beautiful. Like the ocean is giving us a piece of her heart. I think it's meant for you, the one who knows and understands her."

"I think she's sharing her heart with you in hopes you'll stay in Edisto."

"I just might. Edisto holds a lot of attraction for me."

He turned to face her. "I'd like to think I'm one of the attractions."

Looking down at the glass, she said, "You are."

He cupped her chin and bent to kiss her, and she warmly kissed him back. He pulled back and looked her in the eyes for a long moment, then took her hand again and started walking. She tried to hand him the sea glass, but he refused. She said, "On the night you may've made a commitment to spend your life on the ocean and you find a piece of her heart? I think she wants you to have it and keep it. I think she wants you to come back to her and hopes you won't break her heart."

"I'm not a heartbreaker, Jules."

"Oh, I know that, but she needs to know it. You hang onto it."

"Okay. I think I know what to do with it," and he tucked it in his pocket.

The moon was high in the sky when they returned. Matt was sitting on the veranda alone, and when Jules and Ethan stepped up on the veranda he said, "Hey guys," to let them know he was there.

Jules said, "Hey Matt, what are you doing out here alone?"

"Oh, just watching the moon and thinking about Jess."

"Miss her?"

"We talked this morning for a long time, but I still miss her. I can't wait for her to come home."

Ethan said, "Well, I have to get up early tomorrow, unlike you two vacationers."

"You know most of the country is off tomorrow?"

"Yeah, I want to get in some work first thing, then take the rest of the day off."

He pulled on Jules' hand to bring her a step closer, then leaned in and gave her a long kiss. "Goodnight, my girl."

"Goodnight, Ethan." She watched him leave down the stairs. He turned around and quietly said goodnight again, and she quietly answered.

She stretched out on the lounger beside Matt. He was quiet a long time. "I gather you like Ethan?"

"Are you asking as his friend or my big brother?"

"Both."

"Yes, I like Ethan quite a lot. I'm a little scared, though."

"He's a good man. You couldn't pick better."

"You approve?"

"Yes, he has my approval."

"Actually, I think it's more like he picked me."

"He has good taste."

"Thanks, Matt."

"So what has you scared?"

"What if I get a taste of a really good man and his family, then it doesn't work out? That would be bad for both of us, and it would be hard to lose my friendship with everyone."

"Have you prayed about it? God already knows the end from the beginning and can lead you. You know the Psalm 'The Lord Is My Shepherd?' It says He leads us to lush green pastures of abundance and to rest beside the still waters. Talk it over with God and know He has your best interest at heart."

"Where is that in the Bible?"

"Psalm 23."

"Thanks, Matt. I'll do that."

They stayed up quite late talking about Jess. Finally, Jules asked if he was thinking about marrying her. He said he'd been thinking she was the one for some time. And her trip to Africa convinced him. He wanted to ask her while she was visiting Edisto.

Sunday, July 2

Another fun day of surfing. I'm becoming a pretty talented surf bunny.

I seriously love my life here. Just over three weeks now and I think it will be very hard to go back to an office. I look at my beach pendant and think I am a child of this place. I understand why Matt keeps coming back and why Ethan moved back. The more I think about it, I too feel grounded after spending time on the water. It's like it washes me clean of stress, leaving space for life and love. Yes, it will be very hard to go back to work.

I'm kind of honoured Ethan asked for my thoughts on him taking over Greg's business. I'm not sure where the words and ideas came from, but they flowed with a feeling of such rightness. No, that's not exactly true. I think they came from God. I've never had such a thing happen before – have an idea, express it so well, and really know I had it right. Jesus, thank you for giving me your words and wisdom.

It kind of threw me when Ethan shook his head. I thought he was disagreeing with what I said. Then he laughed. I love that laugh. I think he really valued my ideas, or rather, God's ideas. I pray that things work out for him, and thank you, Jesus, for your inspiration.

I felt like I walked in your light today. I was connected to your creation through surfing. Is that the key? Hmm. I don't think so. I think I walked in your light because I chose to think on all that is good. I didn't go into the past in my mind at all today. Is it a matter of controlling my mind? Is it an immersion in your provision, your beautiful world that holds my attention on you and the good things you provide?

Matt said I should pray about Ethan and me. So what is the end? If it's not a good ending, then I'd rather just stay friends. The thing is Ethan is slowly moving our relationship forward. I really enjoy his company. I think he feels the same. Oh God, is this something you are giving to me? Is this the right thing for me? And the right thing for Ethan? I would really love to be a part of this family, but I'd rather not lose their friendship on a gamble that Ethan and I have a workable relationship and both of us want to get married. Married! Am I really thinking about marriage? Not yet. But I don't want to go much further down a relationship path without thinking about the final outcome. Yes, I think he would be a great partner, but the question is, am I willing to risk his friendship? I'd really like to hear from you, God. Is this from you?

So today was a good day. I pray that tomorrow will be good as well. Maybe that's the key. Let Ethan take the lead and just take things one day at a time.

My word for today is Inspiration.

Chapter 22 | Esteem

Monday, July 3

Jules slept in and enjoyed a leisurely breakfast on the veranda. She contemplated the turn of events with Ethan. Her heart skipped a beat. She'd prayed about it before she fell asleep and felt at ease about things, but decided to not think too far ahead. *I can't let my heart think about where this might or might not lead. I need to just take things one day at a time. I don't want to go down the path of jumping in and clinging desperately to a relationship. I'll let it take its course. If it's meant to be, it'll become something great and if not, then my heart and hopes are not on the line.*

Prepared for a full day at the beach, the honeymoon couple greeted her and was on their way. The neighbourhood seemed really quiet and she figured everyone was out precelebrating Independence Day. She settled into reading the fifth book from Ethan and was well into the story when he pulled up.

"Hey my girl. Has everyone gone fishing already?"

"Hey Ethan. Yeah. I think they were out pretty early."

"Do you have any plans for the day?"

"No, not really. I considered going down to the beach, but I suspect it'll be quite busy today. So I thought I might just hang around the house."

"Interested in sailing?"

"Always!"

"Mom and Dad are going out and invited me along, and I'm inviting you."

"Are you sure? It sounds like a close family thing."

"Yes, I'm sure. Both Mom and Dad were glad to hear you might be coming."

"Okay. When are you leaving?"

"As soon as we get to the marina. Mind if we take the Jeep?"

"No. Let me grab the keys. I'll be right back." When she came out and locked up, she tossed him the keys. Once in the Jeep Ethan reached for her hand and kissed it. He looked at her and smiled. "You might be a distraction to me today." He winked at her and shifted into first. She looked out the window and thought she'd come a long way from the black emotional hole she was in three weeks ago.

"Ethan, should we stop and pick up some groceries?"

"Hahaha, Mom said I should tell you not to bring anything but yourself."

He grabbed his pack from the back and they walked hand in hand to the boat. She knew his parents had not missed that detail. Greg said, "Glad you could join us today, Jules. I hope Ethan is going to give us a good sail today."

"I hope so too," she said smiling. "Thank you for letting me tag along again."

Sandra said, "You remind us so much of Peggy. We enjoy having you around. Consider yourself always welcome to join us, dear. Peggy always did."

Greg said, "Well, ladies. Where shall we go today?

Jules shrugged and Sandra said, "How about north up Seabrook and Kiawah way?"

"Upcoast it is."

Ethan took care of the sail covers, bumpers and lines while Greg navigated to the inlet. Once the sails were up and sheets adjusted, he came and sat at the back beside Jules and joined the conversation with his mom.

Jules found it a leisurely day and enjoyed watching the land as it passed by. She was right, there were a lot of people on the beach and in the water. Greg took them a fair distance out to avoid much of the congestion. He asked if Jules would like to take the helm. She looked at Ethan and he nodded for her to go.

Greg gave her some instructions on following a compass reading and left her to pilot. At first he did 360-degree spot checks, but found Ethan had already trained her. If she thought a vessel might come too close, she told Ethan what she thought they should do, then Ethan and Greg crewed the tack change for her. She was having the time of her life.

She heard the family's conversation and didn't feel like she was interfering. Sandra had a book with her that she settled in to read, and Ethan and Greg sat behind her talking. Then she heard something that perked her ears. She noticed Sandra quietly put down her book.

"Dad, I've been thinking about the business and you wanting to semi retire."

"Uh huh."

"I'd like to make a proposition. You know I don't really want too much office work, but I might have a way that would allow me to like the work and you to start to ease off. I enjoy the sailing part and working with people. What would you think if instead of a school open to all the newbie vacationers, we tried an advanced school where I help out mature sailors looking to improve and the serious young guys looking to get into racing. It could be about building skills as well as helping folks learn to get the most out of their boats. And we could offer advanced services and equipment for sailboats. We could still offer the basic services of a marina, but also focus on helping maturing sailors.

"If we see it's a viable venture, could we look for someone who could do the administrative work and you and I provide oversight?

We'd need you more involved at the beginning, but I think over time you could back away from work as much as you wanted and I could take over the supervision aspects of administration. What do you think?"

Jules held her breath, waiting to hear Greg's answer. After thinking a moment he said, "Son, I think it's a great idea. I know the men in the club appreciate when they can get some of your time. It wouldn't take long until word was out up and down the coast. I think you have exceptional skill and knowledge, and would really like to see you put it to work.

"The one possible snag is in finding the right management person. I've been looking for awhile for someone who could take on some of the work for me, and it's tough finding someone capable, yet willing to work under supervision. They need to be autonomous and fully transparent, ethical, honest and accountable.

"I hired a guy in his 40s last fall and he had the ability, but didn't want to answer to me. I had to let him go within three months. Nonetheless, I don't think it's a roadblock to giving your plan a try. There's one person I think would work out, but there are a few things that need to fall into place before I want to talk about who it is."

Jules said, "Ethan, there's a speedboat off our starboard coming toward us pretty fast."

Ethan stood up and looked. "He should give way as he's under power, but we'll keep an eye on him. You never know who's out on the water when it comes to national holidays." He stayed beside her to watch. "Man, he's coming fast. Let me take the helm. Dad, can you get the sheets? Let's come hard starboard into broad reach and get to his port side. Helms alee!" He spun the wheel hard and after the boom swung over the cockpit, he asked Jules to hold the wheel on the heading and helped his dad with the sails.

They all watched as the boat turned toward them and continued to close in. "Straight out to sea, Jules!" and Ethan started to spin the wheel for her, then quickly adjusted the sails to capture as much wind to move them off its path. Looking at the speedboat he pointed east-southeast and asked Jules to turn a bit farther away from the on-coming boat. Getting all the power he could from the sails, the speed-boat passed them port aft, missing them by a few yards.

Everyone stood to look at the driver as the boat passed, and saw he was alone in the boat and slumped over. Ethan jumped down the galley steps to get the radio mic and called in a Mayday emergency. On such a busy day, the coast guard would not be far off. When he stepped back up to the cockpit, Jules had given the helm back to Greg and was sitting on the edge of the seat at the back. Ethan brought the binoculars up with him and focused on the boat speeding away.

"It looks like his path is clear. Everyone is well out of his way."

Greg pointed to a vessel coming in from the east at top speed. Jules stood up to watch. Ethan looked through the glasses and said, "It's a coast guard cutter."

The cutter closed in on the runaway boat. The guard pulled alongside in a Zodiac and boarded the vessel, quickly powering it down. Ethan handed the glasses to his mom. He looked at Jules and saw she was concerned and perhaps a little frightened. He put his arm around her waist and pulled her to bump hips. "Thanks, Jules. You did a great job."

She looked at him a little wide eyed.

"Yeah, really, my girl. You did terrific."

"I hope he's going to be okay."

"Me too. Jesus, please be with this man and give the coast guard wisdom in treating him."

Greg and Sandra both said, "Amen."

The coast guard called for the *Reckless Abandon* and Ethan went back into the galley and spoke with the dispatcher, giving her their contact information for the inevitable inquiry. Greg turned to Jules and squeezed her shoulder. "Good job spotting him. You held your own, my girl. Well done!"

"Thanks, Greg, but I only did what Ethan told me. He's the hero."

Ethan came back up and Greg put his arm around him, squeez-ing his neck, then patting him on the back. "Quick thinking, Son.

Thank you. I think you just saved us from disaster."

"Thanks, Dad."

Things settled down and Ethan sat beside Jules. He leaned over to whisper in her ear. "You impressed the old man."

"No. *You* impressed the old man."

He sat back and smiled.

She sat back as well. He scooted in closer and rested his arm behind her. The rest of the day passed without further excitement. Jules felt she got to know Greg and Sandra much better. She liked the way they remained Ethan's proud parents, yet they all interacted like good friends. She'd never known or even seen a family like this. Alienation and abandonment had been constant companions for most of her life. Watching these people opened her eyes to a beautiful way of living.

She tucked every moment of the day into her heart as a treasured memory she could recall with fondness, and felt inspired to build a relationship with her poppa. My poppa. She smiled to herself. *Seems I've picked up the practice of using my in front of a word as a term of endearment.* She like the way it confirmed connection.

Monday, July 3

Sailing again today. What a memory treasure. Not just the sailing, but all things together – the water, the sky, the wind, the sails, the speed, the family, the love, appreciation, respect. A moment in life I will tuck away in a special place and remember fondly. Thank you, Jesus, for being with us today. Thank you for your protection.

I admire Ethan for all that he is – all that I've seen him be – world renowned sailor, loving son, cool hero, protector, advisor, faithful brother and friend, growing pillar of the community and the man who wanted to give me the heart of the ocean. I've not known a man like Ethan. That he's taken an interest in me astounds me. What if he gets to know me and then doesn't like me so much?

Okay, I thought I'd decided to take it one day at a time. And this was a good day. Oh God, please help me accept all that you offer and help me be all you want me to be. I have Matt's word that Ethan is a good man, but there was no assurance I won't screw it up with a desperate neediness. Dear Jesus, I need to lean on you. I need your strength. I'll need to be sure of myself before taking too much chance in dating Ethan. Looking at Ethan I know it would be easy to give my heart away. And I want to be sure this is the right thing – your thing.

Oh God, please help me to not make another big mistake in my life. This stepping out of the past and into my present and future is not so easy. I'm a little scared and even more unsure.

My word for today is Esteem.

Chapter 23 | Inner Tranquility

Tuesday July 4, Independence Day

Then next morning Matt and Jules joined Ethan, Ryan and Cass in their kitchen. Everyone waited to hear what Matt arranged for their Independence Day entertainment. "Brad and Jo have invited all of us to go out on the Jet Skis today. We can play in the inlet, or get in some wakeboarding on Harbor River, take in the military flyover and play in the waves. He's got six craft, so a couple of us would need to double up but we could take turns."

Cass said, "That sounds great. I haven't seen Brad and Jo since our class reunion in May." They finished their breakfast and coffees, changed and packed for the day.

They found Brad and Jo already down on the dock. Cass introduced Jules. "Jules, this is Brad and Joanna Preston. Jo and I were inseparable in high school."

Jo said, "Good to meet you Jules."

Brad said, "I hear you're a fairly good Jet Skier. Matt said you were already jumping some good-sized waves."

"And falling off plenty, but we had fun. Good to meet you two and thank you for inviting me along."

Giving Matt a punch on the arm, Brad said, "Matt said we had to because he wasn't allowed out without bringing along his little sister."

Jo said, "Brad! Jules, don't listen to him. He's being a brat because Matt was bragging about his new sister. We've heard a lot about you and wanted you to come."

Squeezing her arm Brad said, "Don't take me too seriously. I'm just bugging Matt. We are glad to have you."

Matt shoved Brad down the dock and they broke into a wrestling match that landed them both in the water, much to the delight of everyone else.

When they got up, Brad said, "Do you guys mind if a couple of you double up?"

Ryan said, "Cass and I can share."

Jules said, "I'm good with riding behind someone."

Ethan said, "I'm fine with doubling up. Whatever works for everyone else."

Matt said, "I think we're all good to take a turn at doubling up, so whatever works for you and Jo."

"Okay, well, we have two machines better suited to experienced riders. How about Matt and I take these machines first. Those two are the two ones for wakeboarding, but still pretty quick and maneuvreable. Then there are the two cruisers. For you guys, maybe a couple of you could double up on one of the Yamaha Cruisers? They're a pretty comfortable ride for two."

Ethan said, "Jules?"

"Sure!"

Brad said, "Great. I think you'll find they all have quite a bit of power, so I think we'll all get a good ride today."

They got into the inlet and Brad headed across to the entrance to Harbor River. In less than ten minutes the river opened up into glassy calm waters. They rigged up a towline behind one of the Jet Skis. Ryan, Matt, Brad, Jo and Ethan each took a turn on the wakeboard. Cass decided to pass. Jules wanted to give it a try and jumped off the Jet Ski. Just as her feet left the deck, Matt yelled, "Jules, your sunglasses!" When she surfaced the glasses were gone. Laughing, she said, "At least they were only drugstore sunglasses. Thanks for trying to warn me, Matt."

Brad gave her some instructions on getting out of the water and on her first try she popped right out. Her snowboarding experience proved to be an advantage. After she had the feel for the board on water, she naturally managed a few one-wake jumps. She glided to a clean stop to the cheers of the gang.

Matt said, "You can chalk up another sport, Jules. That's five now. Six to go."

"Six! I'll either be in the best shape of my life or crippled by the time you finish with me! What else do you have in mind?"

"Well, there's snorkelling, scuba diving, standup paddling, windsurfing, kitesurfing, and parasailing."

"I don't know if the last one counts as a watersport."

"Oh, it counts! It starts and ends on water."

"I can't wait for Jess to get here and you can focus your athletic attention on her for awhile."

"Not to worry. I can handle taking both of you on my adventures."

Laughing at their banter Ethan helped her remove the board and get back onboard the cruiser.

After another couple of rounds of boarding for the others, they dried off and everyone drove along the length of the bay, opening up the machines to top speed. Jules hung onto Ethan. She figured it would probably hurt significantly to fall off at top speed. He called back, "You okay?"

She woohooed at the top of her lungs and the wind almost sucked her breath away. Ethan laughed. "I think you're a closet adrenaline junkie!"

"I think you're right!"

Ethan slowed for a gentle turn back and they circled the bay, playing in their own wake. Jules took a turn by herself, ripping across the water and trying turns at increasing speed. She swapped spots with Ethan and cruised the bay with Matt. He unexpectedly slowed to idle and pointed to the shoreline treetops. "Look!"

She saw a large stick nest and an adult great blue heron landing on the branch. Three young birds stood up at the arrival of their parent. She was surprised at their noise, all squawking for food. She laughed at the young flapping their wings and knocking each other off balance. They watched until the adult flew away and the babies sat back down.

Matt spotted the gang gathering for a break at the far end of the bay and started up to join them. As they bobbed on the water, Cass mentioned her parents' anniversary was a week Friday and she invited everyone to go to her parents' house for a 35th big evening bash.

Jules thought, *That's July 14th.* Without thinking she quietly said, "That's the day before my birthday." A wave of nostalgia for the summer of her 14th birthday washed over her. She missed her grammy and wondered if the sadness of her loss would pervade the day.

Matt glanced back at her. "Your birthday? Really? We'll have to celebrate. Let's plan on going into Charleston for dinner Saturday night."

"I didn't mean to say that out loud. Don't make a big deal out of it. I don't want a big hoo-ha. I'm more of a quiet birthday person."

"Okay, no big deal. I'll keep it to Ethan, Cass, Ryan, you and me. But we *will* be celebrating your birthday."

Ryan said if they wanted to watch the flyover, they should head out to the ocean. Matt and Ethan swapped spots and they drove out between Hunting and Pritchards islands. They got out past the breaking waves and bobbed about, waiting for the military jets. When they saw them coming, they all stood and waved. The jets flew low and in formation to the delight of people up and down the coast. Veterans flying old biplanes followed the jets.

They headed back around 5 p.m. for Brad and Jo to keep a prior evening commitment, stopping for gas at the marina. They thanked them for a great day, then hung out together on Cass and Ryan's back deck until midnight.

Tuesday, July 4

Best Independence Day ever! Imagine Jet Skiing and wake-boarding in one day. How awesome!

Like Matt said, another sport to add to my list. When someone asks how my summer vacation went, I'll have plenty to tell them.

It's been only three weeks here and my life has changed dramatically – almost unbelievably. I feel like a different person – my own person. I'm free to be myself and can exist quite happily without giving up my body and soul to another.

I think about it now and find I am genuinely happy in myself for the first time in my adult life. Thank you, God, for restoring me to life. Thank you for your peace, your life, your light.

My word for today is Inner Tranquility

Chapter 24 | Step of Trust

Wednesday, July 5

The next day Jules stopped in to see Mac after her morning's work for the owner of the property management company. He offered her some lunch, and they went to the kitchen to make roast chicken sandwiches and sweet iced tea. He collected the things from the fridge and she assembled the sandwiches. She smiled at the companionable way he easily brought her into his everyday life. She felt increasingly comfortable with Mac as her poppa and looked forward to her time with him. She loved the way he gently shared his time-earned wisdom.

Mac enjoyed her company and it pleased him enormously that she was comfortable enough to just show up at his door. After that first lunch he made sure to have food supplies ready in case she dropped by. Knowing she wasn't taking him by surprise and unprepared, she often dropped by at lunch. She loved the ordinariness of preparing food and eating together. She had a grandfather.

By midafternoon she was on the beach, and checking on the weeping dune and the stones. It'd been nearly a week since she'd last checked. What she saw caused her to gasp. There were three new stones, but that was not the thing that brought a smile. Carefully placed at the bottom of one was the pink sea glass Ethan had found. She held her hand to her heart as she leaned forward to read it. "In reckless abandon, I feel your joy in skipping across the waves."

There sat the evidence she needed. *It is Ethan! He is the author! I've been charmed by the poet and I've been fascinated by the man. And now I find the two are one.*

She leaned down and touched the sea glass. *I love how the ocean's heart now sits at rest with the ocean-lover's voice. It feels like a symbolic commitment to his new career path.* She looked to the earlier stones to read the related line. "The One who gives a man love of wind and water, spray of the bow and snap of the sail." *In reckless abandon – that's the name of Greg Thomas' boat! A heart given to wind and wave in* Reckless Abandon. *That's perfect!*

She read the other new stones. "Like the roar of waves and the quiet lick against the resting bow" and "In exuberance and in quiet, I praise you for all you are." Then she read the related earlier line. "The One who motivates the sea to dance and sing." She thought about what Ethan wrote. *I think Ethan's like King David in the Bible. His heart is bent to praise God in excitement and in quiet.* She squatted and lifted her hands to heaven like she'd seen people do when worshiping God. *Oh God, teach me to love you like Ethan does. Teach me to praise you in my joy and in my quiet reflective time. I see you through Ethan's eyes and see that you are unimaginably great. Thank you for caring for me.*

She carefully reread the poem, now knowing Ethan was the author. It made sense that it resonated so much with her, as he had come to Edisto when at a crossroads in life just like her. Ethan impressed her more than ever.

She returned to her towel, pondering what to do with her new knowledge. She considered the option of telling him she'd discovered his poem stones, then thought better of it. She decided if it was appropriate he knew, then the opportunity would clearly present itself. For the time being, she would say nothing.

Friday, July 7

A couple of days later, Jules had the morning off and decided to spend it with Mac. "Good morning, my girl. I'm glad you came today. I have a client I've been working with off and on over the years. They're unable to reconcile the year-end and asked for me to take a look. You know the software so well. I think I've found the error, or rather series of errors, but I'd like you to take a look, if you wouldn't mind." They spent the remainder of the morning sorting out the books.

Over lunch Mac asked about her plans for the fall. "I'm not sure. I go back to work after Labour Day. I'm just not sure where I will live. I've moved out of Anders' apartment in New York City, so I'm home-less."

"Are you going to find a place of your own in New York?"

"I don't know. I really don't want to move back there." She stopped eating and looked out to the deck and beyond. "I've enjoyed my time here and I think it'll be hard to leave." She looked back at Mac and smiled. "And I'd miss a lot of people I've now come to care about – like you, Poppa."

"I'll miss you too, my girl."

They ate in silence. When Mac finished, he wiped his mouth with the napkin, stood up, took Jules' hand and they walked out to the deck. "Sit down here. I'd like to talk to you about something."

She looked at his face for insight on how intense this discussion would be. He looked serious and she felt a twinge of anxiety. *The last time we had a serious talk out here, he blew apart what I knew about family. What other big revelation is he going to spring on me?*

Looking her in the eyes, he said, "I've been thinking about life a lot lately. I've worked hard and played some. With my heart attack I think it's time I switch things around. It's time I play hard and work some. Actually I don't need to work. I think I've kept on because the good folks of Edisto need me. But I find I'm less and less enthused about the work.

"And I watch you and think you enjoy it. You care about the people and have the strength of youth. I would like to ask if you'd consider staying on in Edisto and taking over my business. I know this is another out-of-the-blue thing and you'll need to think about it, but I hope you will seriously consider it. For me, I can pass my life's work onto my heir, it keeps you here near me, I know my clients will be well cared for, and I can enjoy retirement. Will you promise to think about it?"

She was stunned. She didn't see this one coming. He was right, she'd need time to think about it. "Oh Poppa. You're too much. Bringing me into your life has been a huge gift to me. This feels –" She looked away for a moment then back at him. "It feels too much. You don't need to give me anything to keep me."

"Oh Jules, no. You've got it all wrong. You'd be doing me a favour, not the other way around. It would be a big load off my mind. Just like your help has been while I'm recovering. I know the work isn't as glamorous as projects, but you seem to enjoy yourself." Looking at her a long moment, he said, "I don't want you to feel obligated, though. I want you to be happy first and foremost." Then with a big grin and twinkling eyes, he said, "But I think living in Edisto would have more of an attraction than just me."

With one eyebrow raised she grinned. "Poppa, you're a cheeky monkey."

He chuckled at her calling him out. "Listen, you think about it and we'll talk about it again next time you come over."

Mac had given her a lot to think about, and once on the beach and alone she settled in to give his proposition some serious thought. In terms of her career, project work was a good stepping-stone toward controller and ultimately Chief Financial Officer. Then she wondered if that was what she really wanted in life. She'd never thought much about her career. She was more focused on her personal life and finding a relationship that would fill the empty void. She no longer felt that void with God now living inside her heart. Or at least she was learning to walk in His life.

So now she stood at a crossroad – pursue a career or choose a more stable, predictable life here in Edisto with friends and family.

Oh, I like the sound of friends and family. I've never been able to say that as an adult. Having just established both friends and family, can I put it all aside to chase a career? It felt like a decision that once she'd chosen one path, the other would be gone forever, never to hold the same potential as it held at that moment.

As a distraction she went to the weeping dune to read over the stone poem. As she neared she immediately noticed the missing sea glass. She ran her fingers through the sand nearby to check if it'd fallen and found nothing. It'd only been a couple of days. *What if someone else knows about this place and stole it? Oh, how could they be so heartless? It's like stealing a piece of artwork. I don't like that someone would take the ocean's heart from Ethan.*

She noticed two new stones and bent to read them. "Occasionally my soul moans low like the wind through the dune grass," and "But you draw me near to your heart with every sorrow." They were placed above the stone that had the sea glass on it.

That's kind of sad. She thought about the first time she heard the weeping dune when they'd come to sell all her grammy owned. She understood the feeling of a soul moaning low, but she hadn't experienced Jesus drawing her into His love then. *It's rather comforting to think if I face that kind of sorrow again, I have His love and comfort. Looking at the stones I didn't know Ethan has something in his life bringing him sorrow. Bad timing for the glass to be stolen if he's got something painful on his heart.*

She decided to walk up the beach to where they'd found the glass and see if she could find another piece. Then she could replace it for him, but she didn't find anything other than damaged shells.

Late in the afternoon she made her way back home. She had just stepped off the beach onto the road home and saw Ethan's truck coming down the street. He pulled up beside her. "Hey Jules. You look like sunshine and water."

Looking down at herself she presumed he was referring to her aqua blue bathing suit and tan. "Thanks. And you look like sawdust and paint."

"Hahaha, I think I'd rather be sunshine and water."

"Me too."

"Hop in. I'll give you a lift back." Once in the seat he said, "Got any plans for tonight?"

"Well, I do. I planned on making dinner and reading on the veranda."

"Ryan and Cass have gone into Charleston overnight, so I'm on my own. I'm making barbequed quesadilla pizza tonight. Would you like to join me for dinner?"

"I don't think I've ever had barbequed quesadilla pizza. Are you a good cook?"

"Well, I'm no Heather, but the few things I cook, I'm good."

"Okay. What time? I need to shower off the sand and change."

"Come on over whenever you're ready."

When she arrived Ethan was in the kitchen. She was surprised to see dough rising. She expected a store-bought shell. *He's a man of many talents.* He had a bowl of shredded cheese, and had prepared the vegetables and meat for grilling. "You made your own dough?"

"Would you be impressed if I say yes?"

"Absolutely."

"Honestly, no." Jules laughed. "Mom buys it in Charleston at a bakery, then freezes it for such an occasion as this. Okay, I think everything's ready for the grill." She joined him on the back deck and lounged while he tended the grill.

"Ethan, how do you know the path God would have you take in life?"

"Are you asking for you or for me?"

"For me. Mac asked me today if I would be interested in staying on in Edisto and taking over his business. He thinks he's ready to retire."

"Wow, Jules! It sounds like you and Mac are building a good relationship." He thought, Oh, thank you, God! What he wanted to say was "That's fantastic. You accepted his offer, right?" but God had asked him to be as much of a gentleman as Christ was with him, and he'd promised to let God work out the details of bringing Jules into his life. He knew he shouldn't get in the middle and mess it up. So he kept it neutral.

"Yeah, pretty good. I've been over for lunch most days and we talk a lot. He said he doesn't want to pressure me. He wants me to be happy. Kind of like your dad."

"So would doing people's books in Edisto make you happy?"

"It's hard to decide. I love it here and I love the people here. But I've chased relationships in hopes of finding inner peace to no avail. Now I have God, so I don't think I need to desperately seek fulfillment through another person. I guess what I don't know is whether I've never pursued a career because I was too busy with meaningless relationships, or if it was because a big high-powered career just isn't for me. I don't mind the work here, but it's not nearly as challenging and interesting as the project work. But then challenging work isn't everything.

"I don't want to make a wrong decision and lose God or friends and family. On the other hand, I don't want to lose a career God intends for me. I just don't know. What would you do in my shoes?"

"First thing – you'll never lose God. No matter what goofball thing you do, no matter how badly you mess up, He will still love you and hold onto you. I know this firsthand. As for what to do, I don't think I should answer that for you. If I did, I would answer based on my own perspective. This needs to be your decision. Have you asked God for His opinion?"

"Yeah, but how do I know what He has to say? How do you hear His voice? Do you hear Him audibly speak to you?"

"I guess some people have heard an audible voice. Samuel in the Bible did. But for the rest of us, it's nothing like that. It's called His still, small voice. He speaks to you through both your spirit and your mind."

"Then how do you know it's Him?"

"Well, I lay out my options before Him and ask for His direction. So for example, with my decision about Dad's business, I said, 'God, I don't know what is right. I can go work for Dad and build up a business around sailing advice, or I can stay in renovations, or is there something else you would have me do?' Then I wait and inevitably a mental conversation occurs. Then I make a choice and pray for His confirming peace with my choice. And He will either give you peace and a feeling of rightness, or you'll feel uneasy. That's it. It does take faith to trust that the Lord talks through your mind and confirms through your heart. But have you ever felt an urge to take a specific route home or call a certain person?"

"Yeah."

"Well, that's what it's like when God urges you in a direction."

"Okay, I think I get it."

He tended the vegetables and meat on the grill, and started to grill the crust, giving her time to think.

The conversation rolled on into different topics. Once dinner was made, Ethan held her hand to pray and asked for blessing on their meal and God's wisdom for Jules in making her choice. On her first bite of the pizza, she said, "This is fantastic! Is there anything you're not good at, superman?"

"Aside from grilled steak and burgers, this is the end of my culinary ability. And I'm no superman. I am a work in progress, Jules. I have plenty of faults." Winking at her, he said, "I just hide them well."

She laughed. "That, you do. So maybe more of a flawed hero. How about like Indiana Jones?"

"Maybe. We share a dislike of snakes. And I liked his hat so much that I got one for myself years ago in Australia. And of course, I like his two-day stubble." He smiled. "That was my dad's favourite movie. We watched it every time he was in charge of picking the movie. We always kicked up a fuss when he chose Indy. I'd never tell him this, but I secretly liked the Indy movies." They watched a heron fly overhead. "Got any plans this weekend?"

"Nothing special. Did you have something in mind?"

"I promised on Saturday to take a couple of guys out on their boats and help them a bit. Would you like to come along?"

"I love sailing, but I don't want to get in the way of your work."

"Well, for Alistair it would be only him and I, so a third pair of hands would be helpful. And for Lyle, his wife always comes along. She loves sailing, but her hands are pretty arthritic and she prefers if she doesn't crew. So I told them both I might be able to bring an extra crewmember with me. And I would love to have you along."

"Okay. When do we need to leave?"

"I told Lyle we'd meet them on the docks at 8 a.m. tomorrow. We can go out for four hours, then come back grab something to eat, and we meet Alistair at 1 p.m. So it will be a full day. I think if we left here by 7:45, we'd be good."

Lying in bed she thought about what Ethan told her about hearing God's voice. She laid out her choices and all the unknowns, and asked what she should do. A thought popped into her head. "My dearest child, I want the best for you and love you. I have great things planned for the road you and I will travel together. I have put desires in your heart since your youth and I am now fulfilling some of them."

Is this what Ethan was talking about? It didn't sound like something she would normally think. *Is this you God? I want to learn when you speak, but I need to be sure it's not just my imagination.*

"My children know my voice."

Okay, that was not me. Thank you, God. If you are talking about my desires for family, then yes, you have given me a great gift with Poppa, but does that mean I should stay in Edisto?

"Two roads are before you. One will lead you into the fullness of family and one will take you away. What does your heart say?"

Oh Lord, my heart says stay. Tears welled up. To be really honest – she was afraid to even think the thought with God listening to her. It hurt to admit it, even in the privacy of her mind. *I've been without for so long, I'm really afraid of forming attachments, then losing them.*

"Are you ready to trust me?"

Yes.

"I have brought you here to this place. Now step out in the path I lay before you."

She wiped her eyes. *Okay. I may need some help sometimes with the trust part – and the courage part.*

"I am not even a whisper away. Always."

Thank you for everything. It just seems so unbelievable. Good night, God.

Saturday, July 8

The following morning Ethan found her door open and peeked through her screen door. "Hey Jules."

She was putting her breakfast dishes away and invited him in. When finished, she looked at him and laughed. He sported an Indiana Jones fedora. Flicking the brim she said, "Good morning, Indy."

"Good morning, sunshine."

She smiled. *Sunshine and water.* "I think I'm ready to go. Want to take the Jeep?"

"Sure." She tossed him the keys, picked up her borrowed life vest and a new pair of drugstore glasses, and followed him out the door.

Once at the marina he opened her car door, tossed his hat in the back, took his pack and her hand, and they headed to the docks. Alistair came out of the clubhouse as they walked by and the three chatted on the way to the boat.

Over the day she and the men learned about sail trim, effective use of the centre board, ideal helmsman and crew position in various types of heeling forces, and several other things she couldn't remember. She learned it wasn't efficient for the boat to sail heeled way over on its side, but still thought it most exciting.

She watched Ethan interact with Alistair, George and his wife, and admired the way he could be honest in his assessment of people's performance and yet deliver it in a kind and gentle manner. She liked the way he quickly put people at ease with light humour, and thought she could learn from him and apply it to her interaction with her clients, be it project work or bookkeeping. Ethan had a great way of building trust quickly. Whether dealing with people's lives or their money, both required a great deal of trust. She tucked away her observations to consider how to authentically apply them to herself.

Sunday, July 9

The next day she went to church with the lads and Cass. Ethan said because they are a vacation town, people dress casually for church. She had an image of church as a formal affair of suits and dresses, but everyone wore their everyday attire. She wasn't sure about it at first, but found it didn't take away from the way they earnestly worshiped. She loved that people didn't come with pretense or self-importance. They all came as God's children wanting to spend time with Him. She didn't know the music, but loved the way everyone sang with joy – like the love of life she saw at the beach barbeque when everyone sang "Sweet Caroline." On the beach it was the joy of being together, and in church it was the joy of worshiping as God's own.

She listened closely to the minister's message on the courage of the Lord and when the service finished, she sat quietly rereading the verses to commit them to memory while others hung around talking and laughing together. She looked up and watched various groups of people interacting and loved the way these people enjoyed being together. She'd never been a part of a place or community of people like this. It made her think of what God had told her the night before – that He'd brought her to this place and it was time for her to walk this path.

She bowed her head and thanked Him for bringing her there – a community and people she could call her own. A warm sense of belonging filled her heart. She closed her Bible and found Ethan talking about sailing with several people. He noticed her, smiled warmly and introduced her. After greeting the others she reached for his hand. He interlocked his fingers with hers and squeezed her hand in response. This was the first time she'd reached out to him.

Ryan would be returning to Atlanta that evening and he and Cass spent the day together. Ethan invited Jules and Matt to his house. He'd finished the deck work and fully furnished it. They packed for a day of surfing, swimming and relaxing.

While Ethan and Matt were out surfing, Jules thought about Mac's proposition. It was a way of staying in the warmth of family and community, even perhaps a relationship with a good and godly man. She'd taken her first step this morning by reaching out for Ethan. But now all her fears of loss rose up within her. God asked her to trust Him and walk the path He'd laid out before her, but she had a lifetime of reasons to be fearful.

Oh God, I don't know if I have the strength to face my fears. I so badly want to be a part of a family that loves me, but my history says I'm not worth Mac's love, let alone Ethan's attention. I'm really scared to take all these steps and accept Mac's offer – of living here. If I accept and move here, then I will need to figure out this thing with Ethan. Oh, today's going to be a bad day. Here comes the darkness with fear charging in the lead. I want to run away for fear he will discover I'm damaged goods and not worth it. I don't think I could bear the loss after committing. God, I don't think I have enough within me to accept your package gift. I don't know if I have the courage to walk this path.

She sat a long moment, looking at the guys surfing, but not seeing. Her heart ached in anticipation of walking away from all she loved in this place. Her emotions swirled about in a rising turmoil. She took a deep breath. She didn't want to live in this all too familiar chaotic and painful world. The dark pain felt particularly raw after having stepped into the light. *Oh God, I can't live with this pain again – I don't want to live in the darkness. I need your help. I just can't do this on my own.*

"I know you, my child. I formed you in your mother's womb. I gave you all you have and all you are. Yes, you are weak. I will give you my strength. You are scared. I will give you faith. You are lonely. I will fill your life with family and friends who will stand with you. You have a marred history. I will give you a victorious future. Come, hold onto me. Rise up. Take the first step with me."

What was the verse in the book of Joshua the minister spoke of? "This is my command—be strong and courageous! Do not be afraid or discouraged. For the Lord your God is with you wherever you go."

It is comforting that God is with me. Oh and there was that good verse from the Psalms that said, "But when I am afraid, I will put my trust in you. I praise God for what he has promised. I trust in God, so why should I be afraid? What can mere mortals do to me?"

So, if I understand what these verses say, I need to thank you for your promises, trust will come and I won't need to be afraid? Well, I can't begin to thank you enough for your promise of love and belonging – to you forever, and to family and friends here in Edisto. You really know my heart because that is all I've ever wanted. For me, this is the best gift I could receive, and I now choose to take you at your word and believe you'll give me the strength and trust to walk this beautiful, bright path. Thank you, Jesus, for saving me and giving a life in the light. I don't ever want to go back to the dark, lonely life of my past. Help me to hang onto you.

Joy filled her being. She felt something like adrenaline coursing through her body. In her mind she turned to embrace a new life in Edisto and all it promised. The day seemed lighter, the sun brighter and the wind warmer, the fragrance in the air sweeter, the sway of the dune grass more rhythmical, and the water more inviting. God's day and life in Edisto called to her. She thought of Ethan's words on the stones. For her that afternoon the sea danced and sang. And the ocean reflected her newfound joy.

Thank you, Jesus, for your strength and courage. Each day help me to take that day's step on your path. Thank you for trust enough for today.

She noticed the guys coming in and pulled out the water bottles, peaches and paper towels she'd brought along. After their snack the three spent the remainder of the afternoon in the ocean. It was the first time she'd managed to catch the waves on her own without one of the guys pushing her board for momentum. She loved the freedom of the wave and the sense of accomplishment of conquering it on her own. Having made a commitment to God's path, it was her happiest day since returning to Edisto. After one long successful ride, she thought, *My life with God is like surfing. I've decided to ride the face*

195

of life's wave on God's surfboard, on the course He's prepared for me. She smiled. *Ethan would be amused to hear this thought. He probably thinks of life as sailing on God's boat.*

That evening in bed she thought about the brief occurrence of darkness.

Sunday, July 9

I had a setback today. Those old desperate feelings came back for a visit. In God's peace and light, I'd forgotten how painful those emotions are. I'm learning to walk with Him though. God has given me strength and trust to take each day at a time and journey on His prescribed path.

I need to remember to thank God for His promises and He will give me all I need to follow Him. Since then, I've remained at peace with my decision to stay in Edisto and take on Poppa's work.

It would've been hard to go back to a 9 to 5 job after such a great summer.

Truthfully, the lifestyle in Edisto suits me. When I think about it, I realize I never enjoyed living in New York City. No, I was made for the life of small community and warm friends, not the cold, lonely life in the city. I was made for life on the water. I love the sports. I love the sound of water and the breezes. Yes, it is good I'm staying.

My word for today is Trust.

Chapter 25 | Commitment

Monday, July 10

The next morning she called her work to discuss her plans to move to Edisto and work in her grandfather's accounting business. Her boss was disappointed to lose her from their projects, and asked if she would consider offering her expertise to their clients on a contract basis. They discussed what that would look like and the time commitment. They settled on contracting her as an accountant architect to be involved in planning their more complex implementations, and providing the occasional ad hoc advising for other projects. Jules was pleased with this outcome. She could spend most of her time in Edisto, but still inject a bit of challenging work into her life.

She looked forward to having lunch with Mac and giving him the news, but as she thought about it more, she decided to invite the three most important and influential men in her life out for dinner. She wanted to celebrate with Mac her poppa, Matt her adopted brother and Ethan her – she wasn't sure what Ethan was to her, but she knew he was important. She called Mac and invited him to Grover's that night. She said she had a surprise for him. Curious, he accepted. He hoped it would be her acceptance of his business proposal.

She then called Ethan on his cell. She knew he was working on a kitchen for a couple and would want advance notice to get home and get ready. They made arrangements to meet at her apartment by 5:45.

Next she knocked on Matt's door. He called for her to come in. He was talking to Jess and invited her to sit and talk with her. The women talked for a few minutes then Jules gave the computer back to Matt. She asked if Matt would come find her when he was done.

Half an hour later Matt came by. "Hey Jules. I was going to come look for you this morning anyway. Want to go into Charleston with me today? I'd like your help with something."

"Could we be back by 5:30? I've made arrangements to take Mac and Ethan out for dinner and wanted you to join us. I have a surprise I'd like to share with you guys."

"Yes, no problem, and I'd love to have dinner with you all. A surprise, huh? What's up?

"Oh, I can't tell you. It'll spoil the surprise."

"So, you are an international woman of mystery."

"Hahaha, yeah, I guess so. But then you're a man of mystery today too. What do you want my help with?"

"I've decided to ask Jess to marry me when she's here on vacation. I have an idea of the sort of ring I'd like to buy, but I'd like your opinion. You two are a lot alike and I don't want to give her something she's not going to love."

"Oh Matt, I'm so happy for you and Jess. This is great news! I think she'll love any ring you give her, but sure, I'll come along and tell you what I think."

They looked over many rings at several stores. Jules quickly got an idea of what Matt wanted. He was getting a bit discouraged that he wasn't finding the exact thing he had in mind. At the fifth store she called him over to look at a set. "I think they're stunning and might be what you have in mind."

"Oh, yeah. I like those! It's not quite what I had in mind, but I do like them. Do you think they'd suit Jess?"

"Most definitely. They are gorgeous."

He asked to see them and asked Jules to try them on. After seeing them on her, he decided these would be the ones. As she gave the rings back to the lady serving them she thought Jess was one lucky lady. Matt said he wanted to think of something romantic and meaningful to do for when he proposed. He wasn't sure what that'd be or when he would propose, so he asked Jules to keep it to herself.

They had a bit of time before they needed to head back, so she suggested they look for an anniversary present for Greg and Sandra's party. They stood for a few minutes discussing what to get. She asked Matt if they collected anything, if they had any hobbies or things they liked in particular. He said they loved sailing and having friends over for barbeques on their deck. They weren't coming up with any ideas and decided to wander the mall. They stopped at a store selling artwork. They came across three pieces of mosaic-tiled artwork of jellyfish in beautiful metallic blues and greys. They both liked the work. She thought they might be nice outside if Greg and Sandra had a place they could hang them on as decoration for the deck. He said Greg had recently added side walls to the deck in panels that decreased in height toward the ocean. He thought the artwork would look great there. They went together on the gift and purchased all three.

While at the card store, she picked up three thank you cards. They loaded the artwork into the backseat and when Matt held the door for her, she turned and hugged him. He asked what had brought that on. She told him she was really happy for her big brother.

When they got back home, she had about an hour before they'd need to leave for the restaurant – just enough time to write her thoughts of what each of the three men meant to her. On Mac's she wrote of family, his warm heart, open arms and wisdom of the years. On Matt's she wrote of the lost boy who had grown into a fun, caring, fine upstanding man she was proud to call her brother. On Ethan's she wrote of a man with the soul of a poet, a generous heart, and a respected and talented man she was honoured to call her friend.

Once they'd ordered their meals, she told them they had each impacted her life, giving her intangible things she'd never had, but always longed for. She explained about the path she felt God was leading her on, and that she'd decided to stay in Edisto, helping Mac with his business, letting him retire. And she told of her arrangements to move to occasional contract work with her current employer. Then she gave them her cards and asked them to read them later, but she wanted them each to know how meaningful they'd each been in making her decision.

Mac was more than pleased to have her stay and thanked her several times over the meal. Matt stood her up and gave her a big hug, saying, "A good day for both of us, huh? I'm really glad I won't have to go to New York to see you."

When she sat back down, Ethan leaned in and kissed her cheek. They looked at each other a long moment. Quietly, he said, "I'm really glad for you, Jules. I'm happy you've found life here. And I'm very happy you're not leaving."

"Me too."

She was tired that evening and had one last thought before drifting off. *I've never had a good man in my life and now I have three remarkable men. Thank you, Jesus.*

Chapter 26 | Harmony

Tuesday, July 11

For the remainder of the week she didn't see much of Cass as she was busy helping her mom get ready for the party on Friday. Jules spent three mornings doing bookkeeping and one with Mac.

She hadn't seen Matt all day Tuesday and went alone to the beach to read. She dropped by to check on the poem stones. To her delight there was a new one. "You refresh your artistry with every tide, every moonrise and every sunrise." It was placed between the two new lines about the Lord drawing Ethan near in his sorrow and above the lines about skipping the waves in reckless abandon. Reading through all the lines she felt he indeed had a sorrow in his heart, but he was rising above it, focused on all the good things the Lord did every day to make his life full of beauty and enjoyment.

Climbing into bed she thought about the stone poem. *It's interesting how Ethan is free to express his sorrow and joy to God. He talks to God about everything – not just the times of joy and times of appreciation, but also moments of need and desperation. I like the line about every sunrise and moonrise. It suggests not just daily, but with the cyclical ebb and flow of life. Yes, life and feelings do ebb and flow. I like*

201

that I can come to you, God, when I'm flowing with joy and ebbing in fear, and you love me and help me.

I will remember to always pursue that kind of relationship with you God. Not one of just my needs, but to remember to talk to you about the things I enjoy, and the things I appreciate – at my high tide and my low tide.

July 12 and 13

Except for a rainy Wednesday, the remainder of the week passed easily. She stopped at the various real estate and property management companies to look for a place to rent starting in September. They all said the same thing. Nothing now. Maybe in October or November. That was a bit worrisome. She wasn't sure what she'd do. She'd need a proper place to live. She couldn't store her things indefinitely in Ethan's house and her summer rental would not be appropriate for regular life.

After work on Thursday morning, she spent a couple of hours on the beach. She headed straight for the weeping dune. There were two new stones at the end of a long line of 23 stones. "The One who preserves my life and guides my steps" and "My soul, my heart, even the earth seek your presence." She read them again. They had the sound of finality or ending. She moved to the first stones to read the entire poem and noticed a change on the first stone. Instead of the words "My Tribute," it now said, "My Tribute to the One."

Yes, I think Ethan has finished writing his tribute. He seeks the Lord with both his mind and his emotions. It's not just a mental acceptance of God. God wants all of me. That means I can give Him all the pain floating around in my heart and mind, and turn my attention to Him and off my painful past. God, I still have moments when I struggle with that. I guess I'm not very good at this Christian thing. It seems to me I need your help with everything. Please be patient with me while I learn. Thank you for taking me on, and loving me. Help me to love you back. Thank you for showing me your path, but I have to admit I'm worried about where I'm going to live. Again, I need your help. Thank you, Jesus.

She felt that warm confidence she experienced when she decided to move to Edisto. *Thank you, Jesus. I will trust you will provide a place.*

When she got back to her apartment, she added the two final lines of the poem to her bookmark and changed the title. She had written down every line as she discovered them. She tucked it back in her book. Every line carried meaning for her and she felt an attachment to it. Although it was Ethan's and she had no right to have it, she didn't know if the stones would stay there forever for her to visit, and she wanted to preserve the words and thoughts.

She still felt a bit sad about the piece of sea glass being stolen. Ethan hadn't said anything about it going missing and she suspected he might not ever tell her. She was surprised she cared so much about a small piece of broken glass. It carried no value except her sentimental feelings about it. She considered why this was so and concluded it came into Ethan's life just as he decided to get involved in sailing again. His heart truly lay on the waters. It was the perfect symbol of his decision. And now it was gone. She cared because it was a loss to Ethan.

His words about the water, the wind, the sand all resonated with her and certainly the natural assets of Edisto played a part in her decision to stay as well. And even though she'd wanted Ethan to keep the glass, she felt it held a symbolic meaning for her as well. She felt the loss not just for Ethan, but for her as well.

Catching herself lost in thought, she looked at the time. *Just in time to clean up and catch a ride with Matt and Ethan to Ethan's parents' home.* Cass had enlisted them as the house decorating team.

Friday, July 14

She had Friday off. Matt had gone fishing for the day, so she was on her own. She popped in to see Mac, then headed to the beach for a leisurely afternoon. She was in the middle of the last of Ethan's books.

"Hey sunshine."

She looked up. "Hey Indy. Did you duck out early on your boss?"

Laughing, he said, "No, he's a pretty savvy guy. I think he'd catch on pretty quick. I finished up the job and kicked off for the afternoon. I thought I might find you down here. Mind if I join you?"

"Pull up your towel. You didn't bring your surfboard?

"No, it's not too good for surfing today. The wind is wrong and the waves are crashing."

"I haven't seen much of you this week."

"Yeah, I wanted to get that kitchen finished. And I wanted to get the last of the floor-to-ceiling windows installed. I have appliances coming next week and I think I can move in by the end of August. I'll still have a lot of work to do with the addition, but at least I can get out of Cass' hair. Ryan finishes his project soon and would probably enjoy having his house to himself."

"When will you have the addition done?"

"Oh, if all goes to schedule, I hope by Christmas I'll have it closed in and should be sleeping in a new master bedroom. How about you? Where are you going to live?"

"I don't know. I've asked all the realties and property management places in town. None of them has anything available. They say try again in October or November. So I'm not sure what to do. I have prayed about it and I'm open to any suggestions."

"Let me ask around if anyone knows of a place. There may be something available that's not listed. Or sometimes folks go away and want a house sitter. Would that be okay?"

"Sure. That would be perfect. Thanks for your help."

They spent the afternoon talking, napping and floating in the water to cool off. They returned home an hour before they needed to leave for the anniversary party. Jules presumed it would be casual attire as almost everything was, but decided to wear a tropical print sundress she always felt good in. Ethan came by to pick her and Matt up. He whistled when he saw her. "You clean up alright, girl!"

"Thanks, Ethan. You're good for my ego. Is it okay?"

"Yeah, people will be wearing everything from shorts and jeans to business casual."

She slung a small purse over her shoulder and grabbed her keys. "Oh, by the way, it's just you and me. Matt said he'd meet us there. He wasn't sure when he'd be back and didn't want to hold us up. Do you mind if we take the Jeep? Matt's put our present in there." She tossed him the keys.

"No probs. It's a bit more sporty for around town than my truck loaded with construction equipment."

Ethan helped her carry in the three wrapped artworks. They made their way to the long kitchen island where they each picked up a plate of food and a drink. Ethan stopped to chat with Alistair about engines and Jules decided to mingle. She headed to the deck and bumped into Mac and a couple of other men. One was middle aged and the other the young man who hit on her every time she did the bookkeeping work for Greg. Balancing her plate and glass, she gave Mac a quick peck on his cheek. "Good to see you out, Poppa."

"It's good to be getting out. Let me introduce you to Jack Prentiss and Christopher James." She greeted them, acknowledging she already knew Chris.

Mac smiled at her. "Say, you look great, my girl. You'll be turning heads tonight."

Jack said, "He's right. You look out for the young men of Edisto tonight."

Chris took the opportunity to spend some time with her. "I'd be happy to look after you. Just call me sir Galahad."

"Methinks you are more of a black knight in disguise, sir."

The two older men laughed. Jack nodded toward Jules. "She's got you pegged."

Mac said, "That's my girl. I can see I don't need to worry about you."

Jules thought it best to get away from Chris. "Will you excuse me, I'd like to say hello to Greg and Sandra. Good to meet you Jack. And Chris, I bid you farewell and good-bye."

Chris gaped at her as she walked away. Mac noticed and said,

"Careful, lad. She's my granddaughter, so you'd best behave yourself with her or you'll be answering to me."

Jules set her plate down and warmly congratulated both Greg and Sandra as Ethan joined her. Sandra said, "Thank you, Jules. It's been a great 35 years with my best friend." Greg leaned over and gave his wife a kiss.

"Happy anniversary, Mom and Dad. Looks like half the town came."

Sandra said, "Not quite. Maybe a quarter. Jules, you look very pretty tonight."

"Thank you, Sandra."

Greg rested his hand on Ethan's back and said, "Ethan, my boy. Hang onto this lass. She's a keeper."

Looking around at the crowd, Ethan took Jules' hand. "You're right. I'll hang on tight."

Other visitors were pressing in to talk with the guests of honour, so Ethan led Jules away to a couple of empty seats to eat. Jules whispered to Ethan, "I'm starting to think I must normally look really bad."

Laughing, he said, "No, not at all. What makes you say that?"

"Well, everyone I talk to has commented on how I look."

"I've never seen you look bad. It's just that you look particularly stunning tonight."

"Thanks, Ethan." She thought how different Ethan was from Anders. Anders would be pointing out all her flaws and she would feel inadequate. But that's not how the men of Edisto treated their women. It would take her a bit to get used to being admired and not critiqued.

"So, tomorrow is your birthday. Do you have plans for the day?"

"Just dinner with my besties. I normally don't celebrate my birthdays."

"Would you like to go out on the *Reckless Abandon* with me? The forecast looks like a perfect sailing day."

"Sounds like a perfect way to spend my birthday."

They mingled with a number of guests and Jules was surprised at how many people she knew. Between her bookkeeping work, the beach barbeque and Mac's welcome home get-together, she'd met quite a few of the townspeople. Unlike New York City parties where she never knew anyone and felt all the more alone, she liked the comfort of friendship. Maybe some people liked the anonymity of a large metropolis, but she preferred the relaxed atmosphere of a close-knit community.

They joined Matt to watch Greg and Sandra open their gifts. When they got to Matt and Jules' three wrapped artworks, Sandra opened the card and announced, "It's signed, 'from Matt, honourary son, and Jules, his adopted sister.'" She looked over the crowd to spot the gift givers. "There you are. Thank you, my dears."

Greg picked up the first one and was surprised by its weight. "Oh! I was expecting a framed painting. This is heavy! And I see it's a set of three. Here, Sandra. You open this one."

They both opened the larger two. Sandra said, "Oh, they are beautiful! I love the colours. Thank you, Matt and Jules. Greg, we need to find a special place to hang these."

Greg handed over the third one for Sandra to open, and took the other two over to the new deck wall and held it up. The crowd clapped. Sandra commented that it was perfect. Greg set them against the wall and said, "Thanks, kids. They're going to look great here." He came by and kissed Jules on her cheek and gave Matt a warm father-son hug. Jules was pleased they'd found something they both liked.

Friday, July 14

Well, it's been a month since I found my home. My life had been a chaos of inner tumult, and an outer dissonance with my world with Anders in New York. Now, everywhere I see and hear strains of harmony.

I've discovered a love for spending time on the water, and feel connected with myself and my world when I take the time to be on, in and near the water. I wear an artist's rendering of the beach around my neck. Like the reality of my intimate and needed connection to nature, this glass stone rests on my heart, rising and falling with every draw of life.

I watched an egret in the shallows. It stood still for a long time then outstretched its wings and dashed across, catching its prey. I think I'm like that egret. I stood still for a long time, making no progress in life. But I stretched out my wings and came to Edisto alone. I'm moving along a new path. And I've finally caught what has eluded me my whole life – contented happiness. I would not have discovered this life full of God's provision if I hadn't spread my wings to see clearly into the waters of my life.

I've always loved the egrets. I watched one fly overhead on my first day here. Like each state has a state bird, I think the egret is mine.

My word for today is Harmony.

Chapter 27 | Memento

Saturday, July 15

Ethan picked her up around 8:30 a.m. and they stopped at the grocery store for lunch supplies before heading for the marina. They sailed upcoast, finding a quiet inlet to set anchor for lunch. They both had a swim with a large turtle grazing on vegetation on the bottom. Ethan then headed the boat far out to sea, taking turns at the helm.

When they got back at 4 p.m., she found a note on her door. Matt, Ryan, and Cass had already left for Charleston early in the afternoon and would meet them at the restaurant. She had just enough time to get dressed up for dinner. It was her birthday and she wanted to find a dress that was classy and still casual. Now that she had access to all of her clothes, she decided on a dusty blue dress with a tank top, low waist and long flowing material below. With her tan she didn't think she needed much makeup, just a bit of lipstick and she'd be ready to go.

Ethan came to the door while she was finishing up her lipstick in the bathroom. She called for him to come in, saying she was just about ready. When she came out he looked her over. "I didn't think it possible, but you look even better tonight than last night. Jules, you are beautiful."

"Okay?"

"Yes, more than okay. We'd better go or we'll be late."

Offering her keys, she said, "Truck or Jeep?"

"Jeep."

They arrived at the restaurant a few minutes early, but found the others already seated. They ordered their food and drinks, and while they waited Matt set a present on the table in front of Jules, Cass pulled out a card, and Ethan rummaged in his jacket he'd carried in and pulled out a present. She wasn't expecting presents and blushed. Cass said, "Open them!"

She started with Matt's. It was in a clothing box. She shook it and said, "A surfboard?"

"Close!"

She unwrapped it and opened the box. It was her own neoprene life vest. It was in shades of pink and purple. She leaned forward in her chair and tried it on. "It fits perfect, Matt. Thank you very much. I guess I have no excuse to get out of whatever watersports you have in mind."

Laughing, he came over. "Happy birthday, my girl," and kissed her cheek.

"Thanks, Matt." Next she opened the card from Cass and Ryan. Inside there was a photo of a small two-person inflatable boat, with lounging seats, anchor and paddle.

Cass said, "It's for those days that you want to float and read, but don't want to be swept out to sea. It was too big to bring with us. We have it at home."

"Oh, it's awesome! You remembered! It'll be perfect for a lazy afternoon. Thanks, both of you."

Next she opened Ethan's gift. It was a rectangular box about 8 inches long. Inside was a soft bag and inside the bag was a pair of sunglasses. She tried them on. The lenses curved around the sides of her face.

"They are Kaenon Hard Kore sunglasses made for the bright light of the ocean. They're really good for sailing. And there's a strap surfers wear to keep the glasses on."

She looked out the windows. "They are so clear. And they really cut the brightness without making everything seem dark." She shook her head. "And I don't think these will fall off. Thank you very much, Ethan."

Their meals arrived and they enjoyed a leisurely time with good friends.

On the way home, Ethan drove to his house. "I have something else to give you for your birthday."

"Oh Ethan, you've already given me a wonderful gift. That's enough."

"This is something special. It's actually my real gift. Come on." He took her inside and opened the sliding doors to let in the ocean breeze. From his pocket he pulled out a small jewellery box. She looked at it for a long moment. *It can't be an engagement ring. Our relationship certainly isn't there.* She saw Kit's jewellery business logo. She carefully opened it.

Inside was a beautiful silver ring that split into two interwoven passes of stone. One sweep of silver had bars of stone that undulated from blue to green. The other wave passed over the wave of blue and green. It carried a line of pink. It was beautiful. She looked at Ethan.

"It is the pink sea glass we found. I gave it to Kit and asked her to make me a ring where the ocean waves would carry this pink glass, the heart of the ocean. I really love what she's done with it. I hope you do too."

"Oh Ethan. It is beautiful."

"Try it on."

She slipped it on her right ring finger. It fit perfectly. "I love it, but it's kind of sad."

"What do you mean?"

"I think it's sad to see the glass cut. It seems as though the ocean's heart was broken intentionally."

"No, not broken. I'm sharing her heart with you. We found it together. It is ours. Listen, I came home not knowing what I wanted to do with the rest of my life. And at the restaurant the other day, you laid my life before me and pointed me in the direction of my passion. You showed me the possibilities. Then the ocean gave us her heart. This is ours, Jules. I may not have said much, but this little piece of glass has meant so much to me. It represents your future and my future here in Edisto. I wanted to do something special with it for both you and me."

"But this is just for me. What about you?"

He pulled out another box with Kit's logo. "If you are okay sharing the ocean's heart with me, I had Kit make me a ring as well. I wanted it to incorporate a pink stone, the waves, and still be manly. Here's what she came up with."

He took out a silver band with lines of black in the middle. One of the outside silver bands swept inside like a wave, making room to inset a small piece of the sea glass.

"Oh, I like yours as well. They're both beautiful works of art."

"I want to share my love and passion for the ocean with you. You've encouraged me to renew my life with it. You said this was the ocean's heart and she was giving it to me. Well, she gave it to both of us."

"Let me see yours on." He put it on his left little finger. They held out their hands. She thought the rings were beautiful, but even more so because of all they represented.

He laid his hand flat to hers, clinked the rings, then interlaced his fingers with hers and they walked out to the deck loungers. They sat back quietly, watching moonlight dance on the water for awhile.

"Ethan, can I ask you a personal question?"

"Sure."

"You don't need to answer if you don't want."

He smiled. "Go ahead and ask."

"Why did you leave racing? Why did you become a minister? You just don't seem like the kind of guy to be a minister. You seem so natural on the water."

212

He was quiet. She looked at him. "It's okay if it's too personal."

"No. I'd like to tell you. It's just that I haven't spoken of these things to anyone. Not even my family."

"Ethan, you don't need to tell me. It's okay. Just forget I asked."

"No, Jules. It's time I talked about it and I can't think of anyone better to share it with."

He took a deep sigh. "The last racing season, in fact it was just coming up on the last race of the season, a buddy from another team and I went to the bar one night. He had just lost his sister to leukemia and was having a tough time. He asked what I thought happens to people after death. I had drifted a fair way from my faith and was embarrassed to share my beliefs – my faith. I wasn't living in such a way that I was a testimony and shied away from sharing what I believed. I could tell he was really seeking the truth of life and death and of God. I didn't say anything to him at all about God or salvation. Instead, I ordered more drinks.

"The race was a couple of days later. We were gaining from behind when his captain ordered a tack change. These were racing vessels with wing sails or airfoils. They're kind of like hard airplane wings. Anyway, when he called the tack change, the hydraulics failed and the sail didn't adjust. The wind flipped their boat and my friend was trapped underneath. They didn't get to him in time. He died.

"He died not knowing there was a God who loved him. He died not knowing salvation." His voice cracked. He took another deep breath. She sat up on the edge of her chair and took his hand. He gripped her hand but continued staring out to sea. She quietly waited.

He looked at her and nodded. "We won the race. Normally I would get a high from the win, but it all seemed hollow – meaningless. I stuck out the celebrations because I was the captain, but as soon as I could, I got out of there. I left the whole racing scene. I went to New Zealand for several months, picking up odd jobs. The guilt overwhelmed me and I needed to escape it. I soon discovered I would not find an escape there or anywhere else.

"I was brought to my knees to ask God for forgiveness. And He did. I don't think I understood it until the other day at the restaurant when you shared your thoughts about me. But the truth is, I never forgave myself. I thought I wanted to go into ministry, but as I look at things today, I realize I went into ministry to work off what I thought was a debt to God.

"Anyway, I'd decided going into the ministry was what I needed to do with my life. Part of my penance was I gave up racing, sailing and the ocean. Maybe I couldn't face the memories. I don't know.

"I met a girl from the hills of Tennessee who wanted nothing to do with the ocean or water. I thought she loved me and I was determined to love her despite the fact that we had little in common. Looking back, I see that neither of us were happy and really shouldn't have married. When we hit Texas, she found herself a rich man's son. And so ended our marriage. And all I had constructed around me as an atonement – the ministry, the marriage – disappeared when she walked out. I had nothing left. No passion for the ministry. No wife. No marriage."

He turned in his chair to face her. "I came home broken inside. But here, God and I finally met on an intimate basis. I finally realized I'd been forgiven. I've grown in such a deep relationship with the Lord. I think I could never have found this without all the grief and pain to drive me to my knees before Him, a broken man.

"What you said at the restaurant really hit the mark for me. It's like a light turned on and I saw things I hadn't realized about myself and my decisions. I don't know why I didn't see it before, but it's very clear now. I see how I thought going into the ministry and doing the work of God was what He wanted. And all along all He wanted was my heart and then He'd fulfill the desires He'd placed in me. He could only do that when I gave my complete life to Him. And since I've done that when I returned broken, He's opening the door to my dream.

I've come to realize God is not only the author and finisher of our faith, He's also the author of our desires. And He brought me here to be the finisher of the desires He placed in me.

"I can't thank you enough for what you said. I think God gave you the exact words to reach me." Taking a hold of her other hand, he looked into her eyes. "Thank you, Jules, for saying what I needed to hear. You opened my eyes to the fact that when I went into the ministry, I hadn't put God first in my life. I had put His work first. And that's not what He wants. You showed me the door that God was actually holding open for me. I was too afraid to step through because of my past. I don't know if I could step through the door to life on the ocean only to face losing the ocean a second time. But you illuminated the truth of myself to me.

"For me, my ring represents all of this – my redemption, God's work in me, my future and my passion. When I look at it, when I feel it on my finger, I'm reminded to put God first, then to celebrate the life He's given me to live. I've come home to where I belong, and now I see the beauty and greatness of God here more than any other place.

"I also see these same things happening for you here in Edisto. I know you love the water too. You've discovered family and friends. I know you've given your life again to God. So I hope your ring comes to represent all these things – your redemption, God's work in you, your future, hopes and dreams – for you too."

"Ethan, you have a poet's heart. I love the way you're deeply re-flective and see things in a beautiful way. And you express yourself so eloquently. Thank you for giving me more than just a ring with a piece of glass, but something that represents all God's goodness in my life. And I've received this reminder from the sweetest man I know. Thank you so much." She bit her lip and looked out to sea. "This will never be just a ring."

They sat taking in the quiet of night. They silently watched a man with his dog go by. Awhile later a young couple in love came along. Then an older couple strolled by still holding hands. Jules felt for her ring with her thumb. She would never forget this night, this time, this place, this God, and this man who wrapped it all up in a small re-membrance on her finger.

When he took her home, he walked her to her apartment. She unlocked and opened the door. She turned to face him. "Thank you for sharing your story with me. I'm glad you've become the person you are today, but I'm sorry you went through so much pain."

"I could say the same for you. But that's what brings us into a right relationship with God. So don't feel sorry for either you or me. God takes all the bad and turns it for good."

"True. Thank you for my best birthday ever."

He pulled her into his arms. "You're welcome." He gently kissed her. And she melted.

"I've wanted to do that for some time now." He brushed stray hair from her face, cupped her head and bent to kiss her again. "Good night, my sunshine."

"Goodnight, my Indy."

One more kiss and he headed home. She closed the door and sat on her bed a long time, looking at the ring and thinking about the changes in Ethan's life, and the changes in hers.

She opened her Bible to Psalm 26. She'd read one psalm every day since she'd bought her Bible. Right in verse 3 David says he's constantly aware of God's unwavering love. She knew exactly how he felt. Now that she was God's own, she'd experienced His love in all areas of her life. She looked at her ring. *Thank you, God, for giving me a loving grandfather, good Christian friends, a job that will allow me to stay and grow in my walk with you.* She opened her eyes and scanned the psalm, then reading the 9th verse, she closed her eyes again. *Help me to find a place with you every day and love your presence.*

She then turned to the Book of Matthew. At the start of the week, she began adding a chapter in Matthew to her daily reading. She turned to the 6th chapter. She read the part about how to pray a couple of times. She wanted to know the right way.

Then she read about whatever you value or treasure will be the desire of your heart. And where to turn your eyes, what you focus on is where your mind will be. And where your mind is can bring a life of deep darkness. *Oh, how I know that darkness. It says that to avoid the darkness, I need to love and think about the good things of God.* Surrounded by good Christians, she realized God had provided her the environment in which she could think on His good things and her darkness had fled.

She thought about what Ethan had said about getting right with God first, then He gave him the desires He'd placed in his heart. The same thing had happened for her. She gave her life to God and He'd fulfilled her desire for friends and family.

She read the last few verses that said she shouldn't worry for her needs in life – food, clothes and shelter. She bowed her head. "My holy Father in heaven, let your will be fulfilled here in my life as you've laid out. Provide for my needs and forgive me my sins. Help me to forgive Anders and Dad for all the pain they've brought into my life. And like Ethan says, that pain is what brought me to you, so thank you for working good out of all the bad. Help me not to sin and to recognize your guiding and direction for me. In the name of Jesus who died for me, Amen."

She read the last verse again. Good advice. *Don't worry about tomorrow's worries. Today has enough of its own.*

Saturday, July 15 – My Birthday

I've never known a male Christian, let alone had a relationship with one. I'm used to things progressing quickly as evidence a guy liked me. If I'm really honest, it wasn't evidence he liked me but really evidence he wanted me.

I always thought like and want were one and the same. But thinking about it I see they really are two different things. In my previous relationships, I longed for love and security, but that is not what my male partners wanted to give or ever offered me.

I'm used to the first intimate kiss on the first date, not four weeks after meeting. Then after the first date, I'd give my heart only to be disappointed in not receiving the love I longed for.

I now see the truth of my past. God placed in my heart a desire to be truly, purely and sweetly loved. In the past I thought a man's desire for my body would become a love for me and it failed every time. It was built on a lack of understanding that love is not lust and will never be.

Ethan is showing me the path to love. Over the past four weeks, he wanted to be with me, spend time with me, talk with me, not jump into bed with me. I just didn't see his attention for what a beautiful thing it was. He's walking the path of love and we just came to the first intimate kiss.

If I truly examine my feelings, I've been falling in love with him all along. He won my heart with his carefully paced leadership in the development of a godly relationship.

I now wear a ring, his ring, a symbol of water and the love of the ocean. And a symbol of my redemption and a new future. A new life as Jules. A life tied to Edisto – her world and her people.

Thank you, Jesus, for giving me a godly man. Thank you for giving me the desires of my heart.

My word for today is Memento.

Chapter 28 | Kinship

Over the next couple of weeks, she worked during the mornings over at Mac's house. They enjoyed each other's company, always making lunch together and eating on the deck overlooking the water. One morning she brought the key she'd found in her grammy's drawer and showed it to him. He said it was the key he'd given to Peggy. It was to the safety deposit box in Charleston with a copy of his will. The next day they went to the bank and found the will untouched.

Another day she brought over the box of sentimental things her grammy had collected to see if he knew anything about the few mysterious items. She showed him the first sand dollar she brought home to her grammy. He looked in the box, picking out a hippie-type headband. He remembered Peggy wore it during their final summer together. He picked out a dried-out daisy pressed in wax paper. He laughed as he told her about stealing it from a garden to give to Peggy on their first date. He rummaged around and found a dime with a masking tape tag. "This was my phone number. I gave this to Peg so she could always call me." He looked at it a long moment. "Funny, I never got that call. Things would've been very different if I had."

"We have each other now, even though she never made that call."

"You're right, my best girl. Oh look, here's the ring I gave Peggy that last summer. I think she only wore it when she was with me. Say, I have something for you. I'll be right back." He came back with the same small jewellery box he had on the table when he told Jules he was her grandfather. "This is the engagement ring I bought for Peggy when I proposed to her after she'd come back to Edisto. She never accepted it. I'd like you to have it."

It was a beautiful classic ring with a large centre stone, and good-sized stones along the top surface and sides of the band. She was sure it had to have cost thousands of dollars when he'd purchased it, and worth far more now if he were to buy it at current prices.

"Oh Poppa, it's beautiful! But you should keep it. This was between you and Grammy."

"No, my girl. I want you to have it. I offered it to Peggy because I wanted her in my life, but she couldn't find a way through the past to accept me in the present. You are a product of the love we once shared, and like Peggy, you left my life, but now have returned. I asked you to be a part of my life and you accepted. So because you are the beautiful outcome of my love and you've returned, I think you should have it."

She removed her necklace she'd bought from Kit and strung the ring on the chain and put the necklace back on. There, Poppa. You'll always be near my heart along with the water and sand of Edisto."

"I love you, my girl."

"Love you too, Poppa."

They smiled at each other.

"Have you worked out a place to stay?"

"No. All the agencies say they won't have anything until mid- to late fall. Ethan tried asking around to see if there was any place that's not posted, but hasn't found anything. Not sure what I'm going to do just yet. I guess I could ask Cass about extending my stay, but it's a pretty small place to call home. I need something with some space to work."

"I think I can help. I love having you around and we get along well. What would you think about moving in here? I've got more rooms and space than I know what to do with. You could take the bedrooms and den on the west side. It'd be like your own place. You'd have your privacy, and could come and go as you please."

"Oh, wow. I never thought about moving here as a possibility. Are you sure? You've lived on your own a long time. I might be too much of a bother."

"I would love to have a bit of life in the house. It seems so quiet and empty when you aren't here. Not that you'd need to hang out with me all the time. Even when you're working here and I'm in another room, I just like that you're here."

"You've already done so much, Poppa. I'm old enough now to be standing on my own two feet."

"What are families for if not to give you a place to live when you need it?

"It is a very generous offer. Let me think about it."

Later on the beach she thought about their conversation. She gave a quick prayer, asking for wisdom. She didn't want to risk the relationship they'd developed. She thought about Ethan living with Cass, and decided it's not that weird to move in with her family. And Edisto families aren't like the ones she'd known. She'd seen how Greg loved his children as his children, but also respected them as adults. She thought her poppa would be like Greg in that respect. She recalled him deferring to her on several accounting questions, much like Greg had done with Ethan and his sailing expertise.

After much thought she decided to give it a try. If she felt it wasn't working, she could always rent a place as soon as one came available. The next morning she asked Mac if it would be okay if she moved in on a trial basis in September. He was already ready with her own key.

Chapter 29 | Finally Home

One evening as Ethan and Jules strolled hand in hand along the beach, he said he wanted to show her something and headed into the dunes. She knew right away he was leading her to the weeping dune.

"Do you remember on your birthday you said I have a poet's heart?"

"Yes, when you said our rings represent redemption, our future, hopes and dreams."

"No one knows this, but I've tried to capture my feelings in words since coming back to Edisto. I've not thought about it as poetry. But you got me thinking these thoughts are actually poetry. Over the summer I wrote these thoughts on stones. There were a number of guys in the Old Testament who put stones of remembrance to mark big things God had done in their lives. So I wrote from my heart and put the words on stones. Every few days a new thought would come. I'd roll it around in my head until the wording was just right. Then I'd write them down on a flat stone and place it here in the dunes. They're about how my love for the land is tied to my love for God. I wanted them to be out here in nature – in this land I love – and I wanted them to be facing heaven for God to look down and see that both my heart and mind worship Him.

"So, now I want to show you because you seem to understand me as no other. Look, they're in behind this dune."

She hesitated, unsure if she should admit to knowing about his poetry. "I think I should tell you something."

He stopped and looked back at her.

"I hope this doesn't upset you, but I already know about the stones. I discovered them the first week I was here and came back often to check for new ones. I have loved the words and each stone spoke to me. I loved the poem and the heart that could feel and write such words. I didn't mean to intrude. It's just that I couldn't resist coming to read them. I didn't know it was you until I saw the pink sea glass placed on one of the stones.

"Please don't be upset with me. But oh, you captured so much of what I felt and put it into words for me. I learned from these words about God and about my relationship with Him. You made me think about Him as Creator and you showed me how to see Him every-where and thank Him for all that is good in this world. I treasure these stones and this place."

"So, you already know."

She thought he was disappointed.

With the shy smile of a little boy, he said, "You like it?"

"I love it. I think it is beautiful. And I do think you have the heart and thoughts of a poet."

"I wasn't sure if it was any good. I wanted to show you before I threw them all into the water."

"What? You can't! Why would you throw them into the water?"

"I guess I thought they weren't that good, and just a stupid thing I'd done at a time in my life when things were up in the air for me. Now that things have been settled, I thought maybe it was time to return the stones to the ocean and let the water wash them clean of my intervention."

"Oh no, please don't do that. I love them." She read the poem out loud to him.

My Tribute to the One

The One who paints in colour and clouds,
The One who draws out the paths for the wind to follow,
The One who created the ocean as a mirror reflecting the mood
of the day,
The One who motivates the sea to dance and sing,
The One who shapes the dunes to drone a lonesome tune,
The One who sketches on the beach in dark and light sand with
every tide,
The One who gives a man love of wind and water, spray of the
bow and snap of the sail,
I contemplate you and your provision.
My eyes transfixed with the ever-changing palette in the sky,
    I watch the artist paint the transition from day to night.
I stand arms outstretched to feel your caressing wind
    And feel your breath whispering in my ear.
I consider the morning, then look to the ocean to decipher the
day's inclination.
    And then I seek your inclination for my day.
Like the roar of waves and the quiet lick against the resting bow,
    In exuberance and in quiet, I praise you for all you are.
Occasionally my soul moans low like the wind through the dune
grass,
    But you draw me near to your heart with every sorrow.
You refresh your artistry with every tide, every moonrise and every
sunrise.
    In reckless abandon I feel your joy in skipping across the
    waves.
The One who preserves my life and guides my steps,
    My soul, my heart, even the earth seek your presence.

"Ethan, that is beautiful."

With a crooked smile he said, "It sounds pretty good when you read it."

They contemplated it for a moment. Then she said, "Do you know what I think you should do?"

"What's that?"

"I think you should take the stones and place them in order along your dune walkway down to the beach. So when people walk down, they can stop at each stone, read it and consider God. I think that would be really – righteous. They'd still be out in God's creation and facing up to Him."

"Hahaha. 'Righteous.' Nice." He thought for a moment. "You know, that's a good idea. I kind of like it."

They gathered up the 23 stones, putting a few in their pockets and the remaining stones they carried in a sling made from Ethan's shirt. It was dark by the time they got to his house. They placed the stones along the boardwalk several paces apart, so readers would pause to consider them before moving on to the next.

Ethan went inside to get them a drink from the fridge. Jules stood on the deck, looking out to the diamond moonlit waters. She remembered the night when it seemed a dark abyss and she'd longed to live in the light. So much had happened since that night. First she found God, then God gave her the thing she most wanted – friends and family. She wondered how many people looked out on this world from a place of dark loneliness and emptiness that day.

Ethan came out and wrapped his arm around her. "What has you lost in thought?"

"Oh, just thanking God for bringing me to Edisto on a lonely, desperate night and bringing me into the light of life. I've never known such contentedness. When I was a kid, the weeping dune wept with me in a time of deep sorrow.

"But now the dune weeps in joy. All around me I see the provision of God in my life and in my world. My weeping dune sings a steady harmony of love, joy and peace for me. I know I'm home."

Turning her to kiss her, he said, "I thank God He brought you here too."

Epilogue

With a deep sigh Amber slowly closed the book. She looked at the cover. *The Weeping Dune*. She felt as though it was about her – at least the first part. The pilot announced they would be landing shortly. She watched the landscape pass by as she neared her destiny.

Tucking the book in her bag, she wondered if she would find all she'd hoped. A friend had given her the book and she immediately recognized herself. Like the author she too knew loneliness and lived in the same black abyss. For a brief moment she wondered if she'd made a big mistake travelling across the country to Edisto. But the book inspired her to find something better than her current destructive life. She was here to find out if what Jules found in Edisto was real.

She dropped her one bag at the rental and headed for the beach. It was off-season and the beach seemed quiet. She saw only an occasional local. She slowly made her way along the beach, checking every beach house walkway over the dunes. If she found one with the poem stones, then she'd know it was all real.

She'd checked what felt like hundreds of dune walkways and was discouraged. She really needed this to be real. She needed to find a way out of her darkness. Wiping a stray tear she walked to the next walkway. And there it was. A stone. She quickly made her way to the end of the walkway and bent down to look for writing. "My soul, my heart, even the earth seek your presence."

Yes! There it was. The last line of the poem. *It is all real.* She stepped on the walkway to move to the next stone. She knew them all by heart. She soon found herself at the deck of the house. She looked up and saw a woman inside watching her. The woman opened the door.

"I'm sorry to intrude. I was just – you're Jules Thomas, aren't you?"

Jules looked at a young woman in her early 20s carrying her book. Dark circles underlined her red-rimmed eyes. She wore her emptiness like heavy metal armour. "Yes, I am." She offered this stranger to come in and have a seat out of the cool sea breeze.

"Yeah, I thought I recognized you."

"Are you here on vacation?"

She nodded and looked down at her restless hands in her lap.

"Would you like a tea?"

The woman nodded.

Jules poured another cup from the hot kettle.

The woman looked out the window, past the dunes, past the beach, past the world.

Jules recognized the pain.

"I read your book." She bit her lower lip and took a deep breath. "Is it true? I thought if I found the poem stones, I'd know it was all true. I mean, did it really all happen?"

"Yes, it's true." She thought, *this is the third young woman in the past year who landed on my doorstep since the release of my book. If they only knew help is available right where they live. But then maybe this is the ministry God is giving me – to reach others like me.*

"What's your name?"

"I'm Amber – Amber Peltenham. I'm from Colfax, Washington."

"Well, Amber Peltenham from Colfax, Washington. It looks to me like you have come to find a way out of the darkness."

Startled that Jules could read her so well, she said, "I want to know – to know if God is real. I know – all I've known is the dark emptiness. You described exactly how I feel. And I want what you found. I want to know how to find it for myself."

Jules brought out a spare Bible from the stack she now kept for these lost visitors. She shared with her about God and His love for this woman. They talked about what a change had truly taken place in Jules' life, and what Amber would need to do to have God in her life as well. They prayed together as Amber took the brave first step in a walk with Jesus.

They talked for several hours until Jules heard Ethan's truck pull up outside. He came through the door unaware they had a guest. "I'm home, my sunshine."

At the sound of Ethan, Amber grabbed her book and the Bible, darted for the deck and hurried toward the beach.

He gave Jules a kiss and asked who had left in such a hurry.

"Another woman who tried finding fulfillment in the world, only to find herself lost. She read my book and thought she would come here to find out if God is real. She found your poem stones and followed them to our house. I invited her in and we've been talking for the last few hours. I explained about sin and God and we prayed together."

"I'm proud of you. My wife, the author who is helping people change their lives."

"I think it's our story, and it's certainly your poem that drew her in today."

They held each other for a moment and prayed for Amber of Colfax, that God would guide her steps into a new life of light.

THE
END

Thank You

All of us have made mistakes, some worse than others. Remember, no matter how badly we mess up God works all things out for the good for those that love Him. He is the author of unending love and we can be confident that He cares for us – and cares about everything that happens in our lives. Despite our mistakes and poor decisions, He loves us without limit and He is less than a breath away, ready to step in. I hope you found the story encouraging in your walk of faith.

I hope you found *Weeping Dune* an inspiring story. Many people have shared how the story touched their life. I would encourage you to leave a review to help other readers decide on this book! And I love hearing your thoughts.

If you'd like to be notified of new book releases sign up at SerenityMcLean.com/author-updates/

I'm always looking for people interested in reading an advance copy of a book in exchange for an honest review. If that is you, please sign up at SerenityMcLean.com/author-updates/ and I'll be in touch.

You can also visit SerenityMcLean.com for her full list of great fiction.

Other Books in the Heartwarming and Inspiring Collection

The Flawless Life
The Word Guild Award Finalist 2016

Chapter 1

September 22

Grace arrived early at work, as was her habit. Her boss scheduled an early meeting to talk about plans for the upcoming year, so she wanted to gather her thoughts and some papers in preparation.

As she neared her boss' office, she saw him talking to someone, so she stepped back to wait. He spotted her and called her in. As Grace entered, she felt the near-physical impact. This meeting was about her.

She knew the economy had affected the company, but every month management insisted they were finished with laying people off. Yet every month they packaged more people out. One by one the staff reduced, and here, this morning, was her time.

Experienced, they operated quickly. They ripped the bandage off in a matter of seconds, leaving her reeling. They walked her back to her office to gather her purse. The rest would be boxed up and sent to her. They collected her security cards and escorted her out the door. Done. Within ten minutes they completed their deed.

At the elevators she stood. Alone. Jobless.

Her heart pounded so hard, she felt it in her head. Her gut filled with anxiety. She felt sick. Her brain raced. *How will I provide for myself and Mom?* The room swam. *What in the world will I tell Mom?*

How can I tell her I lost my job? They said it was without cause, they didn't think they needed my skill set anymore. But what about the others who got shuffled to new roles? Am I not good enough? What had I done wrong? Why me?

Then the wave of self-recrimination ploughed over. She felt completely worthless. *They don't want or need me anymore.*

Read about how God holds our right hand
and says to you, "Do not be afraid. I'm here to help you."
The Flawless Life is now available both in
paperback and ebook.

Leaving Lost

Chapter 1

She had just enough time to stop and say a final goodbye before catching her flight back home. She stepped out of the car and opened her umbrella. The drizzly, grey day reflected her heart. Looking toward the back of the old church lot, she let out a deep sigh. For two years she'd refused to let go. She navigated through the cemetery to a quiet spot overlooking the River Don. She laid flowers on the grave and sat down cross-legged on the wet grass. It felt like it had been raining for years.

"I'm sorry, Andrew, but I have to leave. I'm probably not ever coming back so –" She choked on her rising sobs. She pulled out a tissue and held it over her eyes. Her heavy heart let out its pain.

Looking up the river she thought, *I'm going to miss this place, but I've held on too long to the past.* She ran her hand over the blades of grass remembering their days together – sweet days of hope and dreams.

Well, those sunny days of love are long gone forever. Death ripped my happily ever after from me.

She looked back at the gravestone, pulling her mind from what could have been back to the present. "Mom needs me now and I have to go. I guess this is goodbye. I love you, Andrew. I always will." She stood up, leaned forward and kissed the stone marker. She turned and walked away from her soul mate…

Read about God's faithfulness
even in the darkest of days
in Leaving Lost.
Now available in paperback and ebook.

White Sands Black Heart

Chapter 1

"I need to have a word with you."

Her heart seized. She heard this only four months ago and her heart was broken. She heard again three weeks ago and her heart was ripped out. And now a third time. She couldn't take any more.

"Yes Mr. Johnson. As soon as I'm finished with a couple of appointments."

Against her will the memory of the children's hospital pressed in. "Your son has a brain tumour. There's nothing we can do." She took a breath and focused on her work.

When she finished with her clients she knocked on the salon's office door. He just let go the manicurist and asked her to handle the appointments. Before she could answer him he said, "Good team players do all it takes for the success of the team."

She looked at him. She thought about her daily struggle to get out of bed. She remembered staring at the empty double bed for countless minutes that morning. Skipping a shower, she picked up a pair of jeans and sweater from the floor. She had to do the laundry, but she'd ignored that thought for two weeks.

She stopped at the closed door in the hallway. She rested her hand on the door knob and wondered how people survived this kind of thing. She looked in. Another empty bed – a little crib with a stuffed horse. Painful memories swirled in her head.

She quietly pulled the door closed and continued to the kitchen.

She opened the fridge – a quart of milk, two brown bananas, and a bag of green fuzzy mush that was once green beans. She looked in the milk carton, thinking she could make a cup of tea, but the lumpy liquid dissuaded her. She put the carton back in the fridge and closed the door.

She had 20 minutes before she needed to catch the bus. She slumped down on a kitchen chair and stared vacantly at the floor. – absent of thought, absent of feeling.

How much more is life going to dish out?

The sound of Mr. Johnson clearing his throat jolted her from her reverie as she refocused on the man sitting across from her – this man who had taken over the business while the owner recovered from surgery.

I'm not a team player? What about the late nights? All the extra shifts? What about helping out when the new girl quit? What about doing all the laundry when this man cancelled the service? This man is a bully and will ruin the business before the owner gets on her feet again.

She drew a deep breath. "Mr. Johnston, I am a team player. I think I've done plenty around here to prove that. But I'm a massage therapist. I know nothing about doing nails."

"You're a woman. You have nails. So what's the problem? You think you're too good for this work? Let me pour you a tall glass of get over it."

"You can't keep pushing people out the door and expect me to pick up the slack."

He shook his head. "I fail to see what Kathleen sees in you. I'm really beginning to doubt her judgment. It's a good thing I'm here to clean up this mess." He sat back in his chair, full of arrogance. "Now, if you don't want this job –"

She looked down at her hand. She silently counted. *One, two, three....* She took stock of her life. *A dead husband. A dead child. A dead heart. And now a dead job. Maybe this is just bad timing, but I don't think I can take any more crap. I'm done. I no longer care. Karma or fate or whatever is in charge – you win. I give up.*

She scraped her chair back and stood up. "I quit." She turned and walked away.

Read about God's love and provision
for a heart afraid to live
in White Sands Black Heart.

Final Moments Series

Have you thought about how crazy things are getting? The young horses of the apocalypse are stomping and snorting. They are galloping on the edges of the world getting ready for their riders to storm across the pages of history.

Rainswept

Mystery. Medical intrigue. Awakening of a lost relationship.

A trail of unexplained deaths and impending environmental collapse lead a beautiful doctor to the shores of the Baja, a suspicious surfer, and a long overdue confrontation with her sister.

Read about when God leads straight into fiery places –
those places we prefer to avoid –
to bring us to healing and restoration

Veiled Agenda

Marina's life takes an exciting turn as she escapes a political coup and faces increasing danger on the trail of Malthusias. Will he succeed in his promise to put an end to her? Or will she finally expose his veiled agenda?

Marina is the target of the one man
determined to eliminate
a quarter of the world's population.
The sickly green horse is warming up.

Don't Forget

Don't forget to check out the free bonus content on my website. If you've been wishing the story didn't end, I have one more chapter entitled *The Proposal*. You can find it on my website at www.serenitymclean.com/weepingbonus/. Use the password 23stones to access..

About the Author

Serenity, born in Ontario, now lives in Western Canada. She spends many, many hours thinking about God, prophesy, eternity and what it will be like. Her life and relationship with God inspires the stories in the Heartwarming and Inspiring Collection. And her thoughts of prophesy spark the stories in the Final Moments series.

As a "pantser" author (writing by the seat of her pants), she doesn't start with an outline, but simply writes the story. When starting, she knows the beginning and how things will look at the end, but everything in the middle reveals itself as she writes. She meets each new character only when they enter the story and wonders what role they will play.

"I don't know if there are many authors like me, but I close my eyes and the story plays out like a video in my head. Then I write down what I've seen."

You can find out more about Serenity on her website at www.serenitymclean.com.

The website shares Serenity's inspiration (music, images, and links) for each of her books, some free short stories, blog posts, a few book reviews, and a scrapbook of web content she likes.

Serenity also connects with readers on FaceBook, even running contests to win a free copy of a book.

Don't forget to sign up to be notified of new releases or become a book reviewer and access bonus content.

Get in touch as she loves to talk about her books, current events and the prophetic timeline. She looks forward to hearing from you.

Connect with Serenity:

Blog: www.serenitymclean.com/blog/

Twitter: https://twitter.com/SerenityMclean_ (note the underscore at the end)

Pinterest: https://www.pinterest.com/mclean3963/

Facebook: www.facebook.com/Serenityauthor

YouTube: https://www.youtube.com/channel/UCt82lzlc7NDix-FAHfuFZXfg

JD Farag

JD is actually a real person living in Kaneohe, Hawaii and is my online pastor. You can find him at <u>www.youtube.com/user/alohabibleprophecy</u>. He is a wonderfully honest and humble guy teaching on the entire Bible. He delivers an important message of hope in these days of global unrest and uncertainty. Each week he uploads videos from his Thursday Bible study, the Sunday service and the Prophesy Update to his YouTube channel. All are great and well worth watching.

If you are wondering *if* you are going to heaven, JD has a good news message for you.

The Good News of Salvation in Jesus Christ

The good news of salvation in Jesus Christ is also known as the Gospel, which means good news, your debt has been paid in full and you've been set free. However, in order for the good news to be good, there must also be bad news to make that good news good. Thus we need the bad news first. So what's the bad news? Thankfully, the Bible is not silent concerning both the bad news and the good news.

The Bad News

> *Romans 3:10. As it is written: "There is no one righteous, not even one...*

> *Romans 3:23. ...for all have sinned and fall short of the glory of God...*

Romans 5:12. Therefore, just as sin entered the world through one man, and death through sin, and in this way death came to all people, because all sinned…

Romans 6:23a. For the wages of sin is death…

John 3:3. Jesus replied, "Very truly I tell you, no one can see the kingdom of God unless they are born again."

The Good News

Romans 6:23b. …but the gift of God is eternal life in Christ Jesus our Lord.

Romans 5:8. But God demonstrates his own love for us in this: While we were still sinners, Christ died for us.

Romans 10:9–10. If you confess with your mouth, "Jesus is Lord," and believe in your heart that God raised him from the dead, you will be saved. For it is with your heart that you believe and are justified, and it is with your mouth that you profess your faith and are saved.

Romans 10:13. "Everyone who calls on the name of the Lord will be saved."

When you fully understand the bad news, you'll want to hear the good news and call on the name of the Lord, confessing with your mouth that "Jesus is Lord," and believing in your heart that God raised Him from the dead. Then, if and when you do this, the Bible promises you will be saved and have everlasting life.

John 3:16. For God so loved the world that he gave his one and only Son, that whoever believes in him shall not perish, but have eternal life.

Here is an example of how you can call on the Lord and accept Jesus Christ's payment for your sin, which He paid for in full with His death on the cross and His resurrection from the dead:

"Dear Lord Jesus, I know I am a sinner. I believe in my heart that You died for my sins, and I confess with my mouth that you rose again from death. I accept you as my Lord and Savior. Thank you for saving me. Amen."

Again, this is only an example of how you can call on the Lord and be saved. This is the most important decision you will ever make. When you make this decision, the Holy Spirit will indwell you and empower you to live a holy life. Then, when He does, you will find you no longer desire the things of your old life. Instead, you'll have a desire to read the Bible, which is the Word of God, and you'll also desire to go to church and fellowship with the people of God, this because you are now born again of the Spirit of God.

JD Farag

Thanks, JD!

If you have accepted Jesus Christ's payment for your sins and now live with Him as your Lord and saviour, both JD and I will see you in heaven! Remember no eye has seen, no ear has heard, nor has it entered into the imagination of any human the great things in store for those who belong to Him. Think big because it will be better than that!

Serenity

www.ingramcontent.com/pod-product-compliance
Lightning Source LLC
Chambersburg PA
CBHW072217170626
46813CB00003B/979